THE SEVEN

3

DARKNESS

Troy Schmidt

With Dan Lynch

THE SEVEN: DARKNESS (Book 3)
Written by Troy Schmidt with Dan Lynch
Copyright © 2024 by Brentwood Press LLC

Just moments before…in *FIRE: BOOK TWO*.

Josh, Maria, Chen, and Hajj returned from the time of Sodom and Gomorrah near the location of Machpelah in Hebron.

Maria was dead, killed by a rocket fired by Bales.

But she was not dead for long.

A mysterious young man from India emerged from the crowd and healed her.

His name—Saleem—and it means "health" according to Hajj.

A new member of The Seven had just arrived.

Josh had just slipped a ring on Maria's finger, a gift he found expressing his love for her, but now this guy entered into her life and gave her the most precious thing one could ever imagine.

Life.

What's the use? Run!

The voice convinced Josh to get away from this situation as fast as he could.

He ran into Hajj's parents, his adversaries who were working with his enemy Dr. Bales. They acted weird, different, saying they had "good news." Something about becoming believers. Josh didn't have time for them.

Josh turned himself into what looked like the local authorities. He was done with the running, espionage and hiding.

THE SEVEN

Then, his world went black.

Josh found himself in police custody. Or were they really the police?

1

Josh sat in darkness under the hood covering his head. He had been transported by car through the streets of Hebron after surrendering to what he thought were the local authorities. They certainly believed they had some authority, pushing him into the car, out of the car, now into a building, a room, and now shoving him into a squeaky seat.

Not very hospitable authority.

His desire was to put an end to this endless running and pursuit to get some normalcy to his life and let the professionals handle the situation. These weren't the professionals he was hoping for. So far, all Josh experienced was unprofessionalism.

Josh wondered if anyone really could handle this problem or wanted to. Time travel was tricky and difficult to explain. Josh had a hard time believing it himself, and he had experienced it twice already. He just didn't want to go through it all again.

People came in and out of the room barking to each other. One thing he noticed about this part of the world—Turkey too—was that it seemed in their language everyone was mad at each other. Confrontational. Josh just wanted a little peace and less arguing, which happened mostly inside his head.

You're doomed. This is a dead end.

There it goes again.

Someone removed the hood covering Josh's head, revealing to him the place they had taken him. It was a cold, shadowy room with old brick walls, lined with metal cabinets filled, presumedly, with information of other police cases they were working on. A single lamp hung over the table where Josh sat across from a darkly bearded man in a blue jump suit.

The bearded man examined a folder in front of him stuffed with crumbled papers..

Wow, I have a folder already, Josh thought.

Josh remembered that the hood came off him somehow, so possibly there was someone behind him. He turned and saw a female guard, with sleeves rolled up way too high on her arms simply to expose her engorged muscles. She looked like a female version of The Rock. Josh smiled at her, thinking that was a friendly thing to do in such a situation. She didn't agree.

Beardo, whose beard was as impressive as this woman's muscles, licked his finger and turned the page on the file in the folder. Josh himself hated to be interrupted when he read so he figured the same courtesy should be extended to Beardo. Beardo took his time and licked another finger and flipped another page. After five minutes, Josh had enough with courtesy.

"Excuse me. Where am I? And, more importantly, who are you? I needed some help so I turned myself in. Are you someone who can help me?"

Beardo looked up slowly and calmly then said something in Arabic or Spanish, Josh wasn't sure. Mrs. Rock behind him snickered, finding Beardo's response funny.

Well, they're having a good time. What kind of authority is this anyway?

"I want to speak to your supervisor or the chief of police or maybe the mayor. How about a governor! Do you have a governor?"

Beardo smiled. Then, in very broken English, replied, "I am the governor."

"Oh, you speak English, good! My name is Josh and I want to turn myself in. I was part of that group who stole the plane in America, crashed it into Turkey, then slipped into Hebron and did all kinds of destruction at Mach … macha … Macarena."

Beardo corrected him. "Machpelah."

Josh nodded. "Yes, that." Now he felt this was getting somewhere. Now they were communicating.

But Beardo returned to the file. More silence. Josh fidgeted. Not this again! He glanced over his shoulder. Mrs. Rock was staring at him, hoping for Josh to make one false move.

Suddenly a thought came to Josh.

I think I made a huge mistake.

Maybe these weren't the people he hoped they would be.

Josh remembered watching Maria come back to life in the arms of the Indian guy. The feelings of relief and joy mixed with jealousy all at once. A confusing emotional brew that sent Josh spiraling out of control. He wanted it all to be over; this nightmare to end. Traveling twice back in time and watching humanity get wiped out each time through torrential rain and merciless fireballs takes a toll on a guy.

You need to look out for yourself.

At that moment of surrender, Josh realized he thought about no one else but himself. Not his dad. Not his friends or Big Mike. Not Maria. Selfishness ruled his every decision so Josh ran … ran to get out and get back to normalcy and remain in one timeline only. The present.

In his tizzy, Josh ran to people who looked like they were in charge. They had that "look," whatever that look is—questioning, studying, dissatisfied, untrustworthy. This is how authority seems to look all the time.

So, he went up to them and turned himself in. In the vehicle, he peered out the tinted glass and saw his friends. They looked disappointed and confused. Betrayed.

Now he had another thought run through his mind.

You really messed up this time.

They all hate you.

Beardo looked up from his files. "Who are you working for?"

Now Josh wondered if he should trust these guys, so he repeated the question back. "Let me ask you something. Who are you working for?"

Mrs. Rock threw a headlock around Josh, choking him. That was a pretty clear sign something was definitely going wrong. Josh tried to say something but the only thing coming out of his mouth was a deep gargle. Beardo motioned his head to Mrs. Rock, and she released Josh. Josh caught his breath, gasping for lost air.

Beardo asked again, "I repeat myself. Who are you working for?"

Josh settled himself back in the chair and took a breath. He leaned in close to Beardo, and feeling abnormally bold, said, "Your mama."

Beardo reacted with shock. He was deeply insulted. He motioned to Mrs. Rock who put Josh into another choke hold. Josh slipped in and out of darkness, shaking his head to regain consciousness. This girl is mean!

Beardo left his seat and positioned himself in front of Josh. Josh now realized the guy was wearing a holster, from which he pulled out a handgun. He set it on the table before Josh as a threat. It certainly got Josh's attention.

"One more time. Who do you work for?" Beardo leaned in so close Josh could smell his breath.

"Did you have onions for dinner?" Josh just wanted to lighten the mood a little then realized he had made a huge mistake. Not everyone had a sense of humor.

As Beardo stood up and raised his hand to slap some sense into Josh, the wall came crashing down. Josh fell backwards into Mrs. Rock's arms. She was out cold, knocked out by a wayward brick. Beardo was on the floor, buried under a file cabinet and the files he so meticulously licked.

As papers fell like snow in the room, Big Mike stepped out of a tank or what felt like a tank. He walked up to Beardo who looked genuinely scared. Big Mike picked up Beardo by his beard, looked him over one more time, then punched him in the face. Beardo was out.

Hajj leaned out the passenger's window. "Did you call for an Uber?"

Josh could see Chen, Maria, and the other guy in the back, all anxiously awaiting him.

Josh couldn't believe his friends went this far to rescue him. Josh jumped in as Big Mike squeezed his big frame behind the wheel. Big Mike threw it into reverse, as the tank-like-SUV backed up, pushing more bricks and papers to the ground.

Big Mike snapped it into drive, and they were gone, passing the already smashed chain-link fence. Josh heard bullets ricocheting off the SUV's frame, but they were inconsequential.

Maria with an obviously worried tone was the first to talk. "Are you okay?"

Josh immediately regretted everything he had done. "I'm sorry guys. I don't know what got into me. I just wanted this craziness to end. And I really don't know why you would come back for me."

"Hey," Chen chimed in. "You're our friend." Everyone agreed.

Josh smiled back, genuinely feeling loved. Now he felt bad for abandoning his friends. "Any idea who they were?"

Big Mike spoke, his eyes on the road. "They go by a name called the Israeli Brotherhood. It means nothing. Just a front for another group Bales organized."

"I could tell they wanted some information."

Big Mike nodded. "Everyone does."

"Were you scared?" Hajj asked.

"Ah, maybe a little, but you're one to ask. You've been in more scary situations than I have. How did you survive them all?"

"I just said to myself, 'Do not be afraid of them; the LORD your God himself will fight for you.' And He always did, usually using you guys to save me. Remember, Josh, when you dressed like a nun? That was the best one."

Hajj and Chen high-fived. As they did, Josh watched the guy from India sitting comfortably next to Maria. He stared at Josh, not angrily or spitefully, but scared. Josh could understand. This was a lot to take in.

Chen, next to him, threw his arm around the guy, "Josh, this is Saleem, and guess what? He's one of us! He got the power of healing on the same day we all got ours! I must say, I'm really glad he's on our team."

Quietly and humbly, Saleem bowed. He replied softly. "Thank you. I'm very honored to be here and so glad you are okay, Josh. Praise God."

Oh great, he's a Christian. Just like Maria. How am I going to compete with that?

Despite all that he did to his friends, Josh was glad he was back with them, wondering as they drove away what adventures were now ahead for all of them.

He quietly hoped it didn't involve time travel.

But so far, it always had.

2

Outside of Hebron, Hajj checked his phone, pointing ahead to some spot and guiding Big Mike to a fruit stand on the side of the road. Everyone got out but no one was saying why. It's like they all knew something.

Of course Josh immediately felt on the outs—again—like everyone was in on a secret and not telling him. It was why he ran in the first place—his instinct or some voice inside him telling him he didn't belong. Josh decided to be patient and let things unfold. He had just run out on them and obviously, in his absence, they had made plans. So just go with it.

Three generations of one family worked the fruit stand, and they were so happy someone stopped to see their display. Josh looked down the rows of baskets. Thankfully they were labeled in English: avocados, bananas, apples, olives, cherries, figs, plums, nectarines, grapes, dates, strawberries, something prickly called *tzabbar*, and two others he had never heard of—persimmon and loquat.

"If you would like to try something, I will buy," a voice over his shoulder said.

Josh thought that was very nice and turned to see the kind couple.

It was Hajj's dad and mom!

Josh steadied himself on the fruit stand but knocked the cherries to the ground. Josh's foot slipped on the crushing cherries and fell backwards. Hajj's dad and mom pressed in closer … to help? to attack?

"Father! Mother!" Hajj cried and ran toward them. They embraced in a warm huddle.

What is going on here? Last time I saw these two they were trying to kill us!

"Josh, this is my mom and dad, Mr. and Mrs. Ahmadi."

"But … we … they … were trying … you …" Josh stumbled, searching for the right words.

"I know this is pretty shocking and sudden, and I need to catch you up," Hajj said as he slipped into his mom's embrace.

"No, I remember now. Just before it all went crazy, I saw them. They said they had good news. Something about receiving the Lord?" Josh remembered his vision.

Hajj's dad smiled big. "Yes, that's right."

"But how?"

Hajj's dad extended a hand to help Josh up. "In the Muslim faith, it is a sin to convert to another faith, especially Christianity. They call it *shirk*. But we saw the way that they wanted me to kill my son despite how important family is in the Muslim faith, but once family decides to love Jesus, they say, 'kill family.' It made no sense."

Hajj's mom couldn't wait to add to that thought. "When Hajj said he had accepted and was going to follow Christ, we started looking into websites and doing research wondering what we had done wrong. But actually, God was working on our hearts, teaching us. We read that God allowed His son to die for our sins and those telling us we had to kill our son were so wrong."

"Our faith says God cannot be one and three at the same time," Hajj's father continued. "But God is God, and He can be anything He wants to be. I don't have to completely understand to believe."

Hajj's mom smiled so kindly. "Now we are one family. The family of Christ."

By now Maria, Chen, Big Mike, and Saleem had joined the huddle, all of them fully briefed on the story update. They all looked pleased at the recent development.

Josh listened but could not react. He didn't trust them. It was too fast. Too convenient. *They'll come to their senses and understand the consequences soon and turn on us*, he was sure.

Hajj's mom hugged Hajj and said, "Now, all we want to do is to walk in obedience to all that the LORD our God has commanded us, so that we may live and prosper and prolong our days in the land."

"Hajj showed us the way," his dad added, putting his arm around his son.

"What do you think, Josh?" Maria said.

Josh felt the question was more like a challenge, forcing him to react. It felt like she said, *What do you think of that, heathen! God's changing lives! Still don't believe?*

"It's great. I'm really glad to have two less people trying to kill us."

The group actually laughed at something Josh felt totally sincere about. These assassins were making life unlivable. The less, the merrier.

"Wasn't the reason that Big Mike adopted you, Hajj, was because of your conversion to Christianity?" Josh asked.

Hajj nodded. "Yes, that's right. Big Mike protected me."

"So now are you going back to your parents?" Josh could tell he asked a hard question.

"Well, there is so much more work to do," Hajj said. "They have become allies and not enemies. In fact, they helped us find out where you were so we could bust you out of there."

"I'm very grateful for that." Josh extended his hand to Hajj's dad, who shook it vigorously then wrapped Josh in a bear hug. This changed the whole mood of the moment.

Hajj's dad turned to the entire group, waving a finger. "One thing you must know. I got close to this Bales' guy when we were making our plans. He cannot be trusted. Nothing that comes from his mouth is good. All of it is wrong and serves only himself."

"We can confirm that," Maria said.

Then Mr. Ahmadi said, "But, I heard someone talking to him about something that may be a clue to his next adventure."

Whoa, this was huge, Mike thought. The group stopped and leaned in.

Hajj's dad looked around, suspiciously, and motioned everyone over to a clearing away from any listening ears. Then he continued. "The man was talking to Bales in Egyptian, which is a different language from Persian, the language I know. But one word was clear, and I heard it. Cairo."

The team took that in, exchanging glances with each other.

"It makes sense. Many relics there. He uses those, yes, to travel?" Saleem had been briefed. How many people now knew about this time travel? Did Hajj's parents know too?

Everyone began playing through possibilities and scenarios in their heads. Big Mike typed on his phone, which meant he was summoning the troops.

Hajj sighed, looking relieved they had a clue, "Thank you, Father and Mother. That is a big help."

"Anything we can do. We are so sorry we were so much trouble," Hajj's mom started to tear up.

Oh, no trouble. Just a few rocket launchers, that's all.

Hajj's dad took Hajj by the shoulder and looked into his eyes. "We don't understand everything or why you are so gifted, but we believe God is a part of this and you need to follow. While you are gone, we will do what we can to grow in our faith. It's a sacrifice to give you up, but it's selfish for us to hold on to you. Go and serve the Lord. We will be okay."

Tears streamed down Hajj's face. Chen's too.

"You will take care of our son?" Hajj's mom pointed at Big Mike.

"He takes care of us!" Chen laughed, bringing a light moment to the heavy goodbye. After a lot of hugs and kisses, they were off again. Josh felt sorry and intrigued for those two who he just recently hated for their murderous ways. Now he ached for them and the way they kept getting separated from their son.

Hajj's dad turned to Big Mike. "We don't understand where you are from or how you finance all of this, but Allah, I mean, God has blessed us with many resources. I want to help you catch this evil man and get Josh's father back." Mr. Ahmadi pulled something out of his pocket and handed it to Big Mike. "Whatever you need to buy, use this. It can't be traced."

Big Mike hesitated long enough that Chen reached in to grab the credit card, but Big Mike slapped his hand away. Big Mike took the card. "Thanks. Just in case."

They piled in the vehicle and drove away, their eyes on Hajj's parents, now alone on the side of the road. Despite their situation, they looked confident and alive.

What is really going on here? Josh wondered.

3

They traveled south from Hebron to a city called Be'er Sheva. The landscape the whole way screamed desert, and Hajj confirmed that fact saying they had traveled through the Negev Desert. Everything on this side of Israel, south of Jerusalem and Bethlehem, started to change into a more desert feel. Everything from the ground to the buildings to the people got browner and browner, covered with dust and sand.

As Josh decompressed during the trip, he listened to Hajj give interesting details about the region. Apparently, Negev was a place well-known to their old friend Abraham, who also traveled through here, without air conditioning, and with his nephew Lot. This land was also crossed by another famous guy that even Josh had heard about—Moses. His entourage walked the Negev south of Be'er Sheva, which can be found around the pointy southern part of Israel, mostly uninhabited, since people prefer the northern fertile land with luxuries such as water.

One hour later, they found a little restaurant off the road and pulled over to eat. The streets were pretty empty. It was a local place with local fare—hummus, tomatoes, falafel, cucumbers—very fresh and very good. Josh realized that he had not eaten in twelve hours nor slept in twenty-four. He was famished and exhausted.

Now as he sat in a place that many would call a dive or a "hole-in-the-wall" in America, but probably looked more like fine dining around here, Josh hunched over his food and tried to pace himself. Everybody sort of broke off into different parts of the restaurant. Big Mike was by himself by the door checking his phone, and Hajj and Chen were chatting and joking like brothers. But Josh's focus was on the reflection in the glass as he watched Maria and Saleem talking in hushed tones the whole time.

Josh was fine sitting by himself pouting that his dream girl had found a perfect match. It was the ideal love story—girl dies, gets resuscitated by a handsome stranger, and boom, she falls in love with her rescuer. It's the stuff dreams are made of. Josh didn't know any of this for sure, but he remembered that moment and could swear he heard the music swell with violins when the once-dead Maria awoke and gazed at Saleem, with his smooth dark brown skin, thick black wavy hair, and blue eyes. And, of course, his faith, which Josh knew was his number one attraction on her list.

Nobody likes you. You should get out of here.

Shut up!

There was that voice again, always trying to separate him and pull him away from the team.

Maria got up and went to the bathroom. After a couple of seconds Saleem walked over to a chair across from Josh.

"May I?" he asked, like a gentleman.

Josh nodded and Saleem took a seat.

"How are you feeling?"

"Good. Tired. So many emotions swirling around."

Saleem nodded, carefully choosing his words. "Yes, your body slips into so many modes—fight, flight—and you don't even know it. It takes a lot of energy in those situations."

"You seem to know a lot about healing and the body. Are you a doctor?"

Chuckling, Saleem shook his head. "No, no. My mother would want me to be one, but no. I took some advanced classes at school and did well, but it wasn't for me."

"What is for you?" Josh really wanted to know Saleem's future intentions. Maybe get married to a fine Christian girl and have children?

"I think I'm being called to be a preacher."

Josh, inside, threw up his hands. Great!

Saleem continued. "I grew up Hindu and worshiped all the idols and gods of their faith. Brahma, Saraswati, Lakshmi, Vishnu, Shiva, Durga, Harihara, and Ardhanarishvara. But a man, a random guy on the streets, older, in his 50s, shared his faith with me and I knew he was right. I just knew. One God. And His name is Jesus."

"And it's easier to pronounce than all those other gods."

"Very much so."

"How many gods are there in Hinduism?"

"Three hundred and thirty million."

Josh nearly slid off his seat. He couldn't imagine 330 million gods filling his head and telling him what to do.

"Hinduism is very confusing. There are six scriptures, such as the Vedas and the Upanishads, so many books it fills up a room. I knew that God would not present Himself so confusing to His people. He would make it simple. Father, Son, and Holy Spirit. That's easy. I get it."

"I'm glad it works for you."

"After the man who told me about Jesus finished talking, he said 'Acknowledge and take to heart this day that the LORD is God in heaven above and on the earth below. There is no other.' I gave my life right then."

"I'm assuming since you are here that something happened to you August 14. What was it?"

Saleem's head sunk. He looked like he didn't want to tell the story. He took a big breath and continued.

"It was a dark day. My father had cancer. Very bad. We were all around his bed waiting for his last moment. Finally, the machine went 'beeeeeeeeeeeep.' And he died. I remember standing there, helpless, nothing I could do. I was a Christian, the only one in my family. They were all chanting, lighting incense, and I just stood there and prayed. I felt something telling me to pray to Jesus out loud so I did. Suddenly something went through my body. From my head to my toe."

"Like electricity."

"Yes, like a shock. I fell forward, right on top of my father and my father suddenly shot to life, gasping for air, he was alive, healed of his cancer. At first I was shocked. Everyone fell backwards and cried. Then I understood—I knew that God had healed him through me as He did through the disciples. I told this to my family, and they believed as well. They gave their lives to Jesus and became Christians and burned their idols and books about Hinduism."

"And your dad?"

"Him as well. He loves Jesus today. He's living his life again."

"Then it wasn't a dark day."

Saleem smiled as he remembered. "No, but seeing your father die is something you don't forget."

Josh understood. He continued to live with that fear that his dad was dead.

"I understand we are looking for your dad right now too. I understand what it is like having him taken away from you, and I pray that God will give him back to you as he did for me."

Josh found himself liking this guy. He was genuine, loving, heartfelt. So frustrating! "How did you eventually find us?"

"Just the other day, the Spirit led me from India to Israel. I booked a flight and left. I found a taxi and it took me to Hebron, which I had only heard of in the Bible, and the taxi dropped me off near where you guys were. I got out of the taxi and saw Hajj get attacked. I healed him then ran away. Then I watched and I realized, yes, these were the people God was leading me to. I showed up just in time and healed Maria."

Saleem turned as Maria exited the bathroom and sat down at her table across the room. Saleem and she exchanged glances, like boyfriend and girlfriend, Josh was convinced, flirting across the room. It so sickened him.

"She is a very nice girl," Saleem sighed.

"Yes, yes she is." Josh stood up to get out of this place, somewhere. There was that flight instinct.

Go, man, run!

Josh just stood there, fighting the flee response, but now standing there awkwardly.

Saleem didn't seem to mind. "Now I am number five, right? There are two more. A total of seven."

"That's what Big Mike told us when the four of us met him."

"How does he know?"

Josh thought for a second. "Good question. Somehow he just knew. His organization? Intel? I don't know. But he's right."

"Well, either way, I am very honored. Very, very honored. I can't believe it. God has a purpose for me. I do not deserve it."

Josh nodded, excused himself and walked away.

Oh, brother, Josh murmured to himself. *He's handsome and humble. No combination is more lethal!*

Josh went outside the restaurant to the SUV tank where Big Mike stood, checking, as always, his phone. "Where to now?"

Big Mike kept his focus on the phone. "We're running an analysis of the electrical grids, waiting for a spike. Bales completely abandoned his last team, and we are questioning the ones that survived right now. They knew about the previous plan, but not the next plan."

"What are you thinking? Where could he be going?"

Big Mike took his eyes off the phone and looked to the night sky. "It's hard to say. We have eyes all over Cairo but we don't know his motive yet, his end game, so it's hard to pinpoint his next move. Right now we are in the heart of where so much of the Bible took place. Jerusalem to the north and Egypt to the West. If Bales is anywhere, it's in this vicinity. He'll need a few days to charge his time machine and find that artifact."

Josh heard a cheer in the distance. "You hear that?"

Even Big Mike perked up. "I did."

Right then Chen, Hajj, Maria, and Saleem stepped out. The cheer erupted again.

Chen looked to the west. "Sounds like a baseball game?"

"Soccer," Hajj replied. "Hapoel Be'er Sheva, a local Israeli team. Very popular. It's probably why nobody is around."

"Can we go?' Josh perked up, desiring a moment of normalcy. "Certainly we will blend in with a crowd."

Big Mike assessed the moment, looking around. After a lot of thinking, he smiled. "Why not?"

"Do we have money for popcorn?" Chen looked like a little kid once again. Big Mike held up the credit card given by Hajj's parents.

The stadium was packed with 10,000 people, most of them Jewish, as Josh observed more yarmulkas than he had ever seen in his life. Hajj enlightened them along the way that this was an Israeli national team and today they were playing Tel Aviv, a big rivalry game. Josh was more focused on the food at first—you can't watch a sports game without food—and found the kosher hot dogs surprisingly good, plus a fountain drink and ice cream! Concessions were surprisingly simple but tasty.

They watched the game and Hapoel Be'er Sheva won 2–1 bringing much joy to the city. People left singing and hugging. Josh could not help being caught up in it all. It felt especially good to not hide, but to be outside with people and enjoying life.

Two things tried to ruin the fun for Josh. One, Saleem and Maria looked cozy together, like he had become the new Josh for her. And second, Big Mike kept walking away. When Big Mike walked away, there was trouble stirring.

Josh walked down the stadium stairs from their nosebleed seats with Hajj and Chen.

Hajj looked at Chen perplexed. "How can you not like soccer?"

Chen defended himself. "It seems so random, like the clock at the end. In what other sport does the referee determine the time? 'Oh, I think I'll add a minute, no, maybe two and 33 seconds.'"

"That makes it more exciting."

"And these flops. Some of these guys should get Academy Awards. They put Lebron to shame."

"Soccer has always been over-the-top, exaggerated fun. That's the way it is. So what game do you prefer?"

Chen smiled, like he was thinking back at the last time he played. "Ping pong."

Hajj rolled his eyes. "What a stereotype."

"I know, right. I'm Chinese, and I like ping pong. But there's a reason we like ping pong … it's good. Fast reflexes. You aim for centimeters. A volley can go for minutes. I love it. And nobody flops when the ball hits them!" Chen was getting worked up, acting out a game against an imaginary rival right in front of them.

Hajj shook his head, while turning to Josh. "Josh, what sport do you like?"

Josh ran some possible lies through his mind. Then decided on the truth, "I don't really like sports."

Chen stopped his volley, joining Hajj's stare. "No sports?"

Josh shrugged it off. "Didn't really have a dad who cared about that stuff so it just trickled down to me."

Hajj waved his finger. "I didn't have a dad who played soccer. You can't use that excuse on me."

Chen agreed with Hajj. "Yeah, my dad never picked up a ping pong paddle. You can't blame everything on a dad."

Maria slipped into the group. "What did you like, Josh, if not sports?"

Oh gosh. The pressure. It took him a couple of seconds, then something very non-competitive and not sweat inducing came to mind. "Going out on my roof at night and looking up at the stars."

Saleem, now also walking up, agreed. "Yes, I do that many times too."

Chen shook his head. "That's so boring."

Josh chuckled. "I guess I'm boring."

Hajj pointed up to the starry night before them. The glow of Be'er Sheva kept the stars from shining through the darkness clearly. "No, the stars are fascinating. Remember, Romans said you will find God in His creation. Star gazing is like God seeking. But if from there you seek the LORD your God, you will find him if you seek him with all your heart and with all your soul. The stars are the gateway to God. Keep looking at them Josh."

Josh appreciated Hajj saving him from accusations of being weak and boring. Josh never understood why he loved the night and looking at the stars. Maybe he was seeking God and finding Him there. Josh never wanted to be an astronomer or starship captain, never really getting into Star Wars. He just wanted to look at the stars—not the world—and rest.

Big Mike took them to the Negev Hotel and everyone got a private room again thanks to Hajj's parents. Josh enjoyed a long hot shower then sat on his balcony before bed, gazing at the stars. Maybe he would find what he was looking for, but not anytime soon.

Josh slept long and hard without a single memorable dream then woke refreshed. Down in the dining area, the group enjoyed a wonderful breakfast of warm bread, salads, soft cheeses, dried fruit, and something like a cinnamon bun. The conversation was light and friendly.

Big Mike's plan was to hang here until evidence moved them north or east. Be'er Sheva was halfway between Jerusalem and Egypt, more or less, an easy drive in either direction.

Josh went back to his room not expecting much ahead in his day except maybe a swim and a couple of naps.

They had nowhere to go and nothing to do all day, until Josh ruined it all with a vision.

5

Josh suddenly could see nothing. He heard terrifying sounds of people screaming, mixed with crashing and tumbling. Josh turned his head left and right and saw nothing but more darkness. It was as if his eyes were permanently sealed shut. Josh stumbled; his arms extended to feel for obstacles in his path. He could move freely and yet had no idea if he approached a cliff or oncoming traffic. Could others see and only he was blind?

Josh felt creatures run past him, possibly nocturnal animals who thrived in this darkness. Then, a hand grabbed him by the ankle and a voice cried, "Help me! Help me! I can't stand this any longer!"

Josh wrestled free and moved forward. In the distance he saw something—a stream of light shining in the darkness off in the horizon. He turned toward it, cautiously taking each step.

He shifted his weight forward before being sure there was solid ground in his path. It was too late. There was no ground in front of him, and he fell ten or fifteen feet splashing into water.

Josh splashed and clawed to the surface then woke to find himself in the hotel pool, fully clothed. Somehow he had walked from his room to the pool deck outside his room.

Chen and Big Mike appeared on the deck shouting at him, "Josh are you okay? Most people don't swim fully clothed!"

Then he saw Maria. That look. She knew what had just happened—he had another vision. Saleem and Hajj got to him first and pulled him from the water. They all convened in Maria's room.

After drying off, Josh prepared to tell them what he experienced. Josh looked around, always cautious that someone else was listening. He knew his words sounded crazy to an outsider unaware of their mission.

"I saw darkness. Well, I didn't see darkness but darkness was all I could see. There was no light and everyone around me was trying to find their way. In the distance I saw a light and tried to move toward it but I fell into a body of water and woke up in the pool."

"I saw you dude," Chen said. "You looked lost as you came out of the hotel, taking each step cautiously then fell headfirst into the pool. It was really weird and kind of funny at the same time." Then Chen smacked his own head, realizing a missed opportunity. "I should have recorded in on my phone."

Hajj immediately knew the direction they had to take. "I think I know what you saw. Darkness … Egypt … you saw the ninth plague, Josh."

"Wait, what? You got all that from the vision?" Chen wondered.

"Yes, the time of Moses when God was preparing to take his people out of Egypt and move them toward the promised land," Saleem added.

Josh needed clarification. "You're talking about the plagues like the Nile turned to blood and a bunch of frogs? Those plagues?"

"Yes, in Exodus there were a total of ten plagues God used to convince Pharaoh to release the Israelites from Egypt. Nile to blood, frogs, gnats, flies, livestock, sickness, livestock sickness, boils, hail, locusts, darkness, and then the last one." Hajj paused as if scared to say it.

Chen helped him. "The death of the firstborn."

Josh paused—did he really just hear that God would send a plague to kill the firstborn children? Whatever … Josh let the conversation continue.

"This all makes sense," Hajj stood, his mind processing thousands of facts. "If Bales can somehow disrupt those plagues and stop Moses, the Jewish faith is done. Those events of the plague are what Passover is all about. It's the most crucial event in Israel's history."

"Even Jesus celebrated Passover," Chen said.

"What sort of physical evidence is there in Egypt that Bales could use to transport himself back in time?" Maria asked.

Hajj thought. "I'm not sure. But Egypt, especially Cairo, is known for its antiquities. They have a museum there with lots of stuff. If I were Bales, I would go there."

Big Mike walked off, pressing out messages on his phone.

Josh knew Hajj was right. It all made sense. It was time.

"Is this how it works? You have a little bit of evidence and you move the whole operation that direction?" Saleem asked.

"Basically, yes," Chen replied, then pointed to Josh. "It usually starts with a vision by this guy that gets everything going in the right direction."

Josh smiled, suddenly feeling valued especially in front of Saleem. Saleem looked back at Josh, genuinely impressed. "That easily is one of the coolest gifts a person could receive."

Josh was taken aback. "Really? You heal people, even bring them back from the dead."

"Well, I don't bring them back from the dead. God heals people through me. He heals the broken parts of them so life can return to their bodies. But I cannot walk into a graveyard like Jesus did and call someone out of their tomb like Lazarus. That was truly a miracle."

Chen, Hajj, and Maria agreed. Josh had no idea who this Lazarus guy was or if he was still alive.

Saleem continued, "I'm not saying my gift doesn't make me feel good inside, but you Josh are being communicated to by God Himself. A message from God, only to you. When did you become a believer?"

The room hushed awkwardly. Saleem slowly felt the shifting of mood. "Is it something I said."

Maria stepped out and put her arm around Josh. "Josh isn't a believer." She paused then added, "Not yet."

Saleem looked perplexed. "But how can he display the gifts if he's not a believer?"

Nobody had a good answer. Hajj attempted one. "Who are we to tell God the rules? Josh has visions and in the past when we followed the clues from his vision they led us to where we needed to go. God simply tells us not to add or subtract from His commands, but keep the ones the Lord has given us."

Josh pointed to the others. "They call it faith."

Saleem quietly processed this revelation and whispered one word: "Cool."

Big Mike returned. "Let's pack up. We're headed to Egypt."

Hajj replied, "Where abouts?"

"Cairo."

"Perfect," Hajj agreed. "And to the Museum of Antiquities, where all of Egypt's prized artifacts are stored."

Josh was sure they would hear more about that as they got closer. Everyone piled in their respective positions. Josh took shotgun next to Hajj and Big Mike. Maria, Saleem, and Chen in the back seat.

As they departed Be'er Sheva, circling another roundabout, Hajj entertained them with more interesting trivia, such as Be'er Sheva has 250 roundabouts, the most in the world. Also, chess is a huge sport with the Israelis here and many chess grandmasters live in the city.

"There's also one other thing I didn't tell you about the city," Hajj continued. "I didn't want you guys to get all freaked out. But the name of Be'er Sheva or Beersheba comes from Genesis 26 when Abraham's men found wells in the area."

Chen shrugged. "So, what's the big deal about that?"

"It's the number of wells that they found. Beersheba means 'seven wells.'"

Everyone quietly took in that information. "Hmm, there's that number seven again, like what we are to become." Chen mumbled. "Cool."

Josh agreed. Maybe it was a sign they would meet another member of the Seven this adventure. Josh hoped so, because number five was giving him all kinds of headaches.

6

The vision was short but it made an impact.

In the darkness, Josh heard the screams of people off in the distance, close by, and right behind him. Then he distinctly heard the voices of two people he knew and loved.

"Josh … Josh …"

It was his mom and dad.

Josh twitched awake but didn't leap through the roof or try to get out of the speeding car, currently in the middle of nowhere. The clock on the dash read "12:03."

He looked around and everyone was asleep, except, of course, Big Mike who stared straight ahead and Maria, of course, who sensed a disturbance. She leaned forward.

"Another vision … darkness?"

"Sorry, I didn't mean to wake you."

"It's okay. What did you see?"

"Not much. I was in darkness so I saw nothing, but I heard screaming and my parents' voices."

"Oh, wow. That's scary. Maybe God just wants to remind you why you are here."

"Maybe. Thankfully, it was short, but something about it was very disturbing. More than what I saw during the flood and the fire from the sky."

"It's supposed to be disturbing. Darkness is the absence of light. In the Bible, it's the symbol for hell."

Josh turned to her, "Do you think I saw hell?"

"No, I think you're seeing the ninth plague, but that plague was probably more horrible to live through than we can imagine. In a sense, it gave you a glimpse into hell."

"Which is where you think I am going ..."

Maria paused, leaning back. "I have no idea, and it's not up to me. I'm just saying the Bible describes hell as darkness. When you have that vision, how does that feel being in darkness?"

"I feel alone ... lost ... confused ... no direction ..."

"That's what hell feels like for everyone there—and it's forever."

"I thought hell was torture, where you got punished for your sins."

Maria leaned in closer to Josh, like she wanted to make sure he heard this. "The Bible describes it as weeping and gnashing of teeth. That's self-torture. Mental anxiety. Worry. Confusion. In a place without God, who is light, people experience all those feelings you felt when you arrived in darkness."

"And you think I'm going there?"

Maria spoke firmly and with lips tightened said, "I tell you this so you won't go there!"

Josh was a little scared by her reaction. He froze, not knowing how to react. "But wait, why did I hear my parents? Are they in hell?"

"Oh I don't think so. I think they were warning you also." Did her voice crack at the end there? Maria fell back in her seat, obviously upset she had let her emotions get the best of her.

"I appreciate your wanting me to be there with you in heaven, but you'll have Saleem to keep you company."

Maria looked really hurt by that. Maybe mad. "You think this is all about having a boyfriend in heaven?"

Hearing her put it that way made Josh feel stupid. Now he had to back out of this. "I'm just saying … you two are getting … close … and I don't blame you." Josh looked at Saleem. He looked asleep. "He's a good-looking guy and he believes in God like you do. Isn't that what you want?"

Maria took a deep breath. She didn't seem very happy with where Josh was going with this. "All I want to do is God's will. We've been called on this mission. I'm not here to find love or get married. The only love I want to express is to love the LORD my God with all my heart and with all my soul and with all my strength. That's the first and greatest commandment. Whatever happens beyond that, happens."

Maria paused, looking deeply into Josh's eyes. He felt examined, his mind probed by her gift of discernment. She then held up her hand. The ring. "This is from you, right?"

Now Josh felt stupid for his attempt to show affection. Josh put the ring of crosses, which he bought from a street vendor before their last time travel, on her finger when he thought she was dead. Now that she was very much alive, it felt awkward.

Maria smiled. "It's very pretty. Thank you. It means a lot."

"I thought I would never see you again," Josh said, glad it was dark and no one could see him blushing.

Josh backed off. He had so much he wanted to say. He still remembered seeing her on her front porch when he first moved in across the street. He remembered the joy in his heart when she pulled up in that classic Mustang and offered him a ride to school. Josh remembered sitting at lunch with her and Chen thinking life was going to be good there if all he had to think about was hanging out with Maria and her family.

Then all this happened. Josh looked at Maria who was staring out the side window. Clearly the conversation was over for now. Josh turned around, thinking it was best to let this all drop and move on. He glanced in the rear-view mirror and caught Saleem's eye looking at him, then closing quickly.

Oh great. Now pretty boy knows everything.

Now Josh couldn't sleep. Big Mike drove quickly—as fast as the car allowed. They were now two hours into the trip, wasting no time. Josh decided to make small talk with this large, mostly silent, man.

"Which way are we going?"

"We're taking the southern route. My sources tell me it's easier to get in and out of the country there, fewer questions down at the southern crossing. This road, 40, goes all the way to the southern tip of Israel to the Gulf of Aqaba. Then we head west on 50 to Cairo, coming in on the eastern side."

"Oh, okay. How long does it take?"

"Seven hours 56 minutes, depending on how long it takes at the border."

"Nice." Josh looked out at the total darkness in this part of Israel, which he had been seeing a lot of recently. No cities or streetlights, no homes, no rest stops. When the sun came up, he expected to see nothing but more nothing—boring desert. "Hey if you need someone to drive, I just got my permit."

Big Mike looked at him. "I'll be fine."

"Of course you will." Josh knew it was dumb to ask. After a moment Josh felt he needed to say something. "You have any advice when it comes to girls?"

Big Mike didn't blink, still staring straight ahead. "I don't involve myself in such matters."

Josh chuckled. "Probably best."

Not wanting to slip into a vision, Josh busied his mind in the route they were taking. At a place called Neot Smader they continued on Route 40 through small towns called Lotan, Ketura, Grofit, Yotvata, Samar, Elifaz, Be'erOra, Eilot and Eilat, a decent sized town—the largest he'd seen since Be'er Sheva. Then Josh saw the sign for Dekel Beach and Dolphin Reef Beach. He was curious. A beach means water. What water were they near?

Then a sign in passing told him: Sea of Aqaba. Josh looked at the time again: "2:21."

A few minutes later they were at the border, approaching Egypt. Josh wondered what Big Mike had in mind. Big Mike always had something in mind but this usually involved things crashing and people getting hurt.

He looked around at the others and everyone was out cold.

"Anything I can do?" Josh wanted to be helpful.

Big Mike applied the brakes, slowing the vehicle down. "Yeah, say goodnight."

Big Mike's hand closed in on Josh's face. Josh smelled something funny and went immediately to sleep.

N ow Josh could smell the coffee and some kind of bread or pastry delightfully waking him up. The others must have smelled it too since they were stirring and looking around.

It was morning. Big Mike sat near the SUV at a table with five large coffees and a dozen flaky pastries on the table. Around them, tourists in beach wear carried their breakfasts to other tables on the patio.

Josh asked himself two questions anyone would ask in this situation—*Where am I, and how did I get here?*

Realizing that food was being served, everyone scampered to snag a coffee cup and grab a bite. Josh was first and had the crispy delight in his mouth when Saleem said, "Let's pray."

Josh choked mid-bite, spitting the biscuit into a napkin, then respectfully bowed.

"Lord, we thank You for this food and for getting us this far. We don't know how You do it or where we're going, but we trust You. Thank You for Mr. Mike getting us this food. In Jesus' name. Amen."

Everyone ate and drank like it was their last meal, except Big Mike who sat and watched.

"Aren't you eating?" Josh asked him.

"Already ate, while you were asleep."

Josh looked around. The place looked like a resort, especially the ten-story hotel next to them. "Where are we?"

"Taba, Egypt."

"We crossed the border?" Josh now remembered the last thing before falling asleep—Big Mike telling him to go to sleep.

"Yes. Everything went fine." Big Mike responded to something on his phone.

"You told me to go to sleep and I did … immediately. How did you do that?"

"I used a sleep gas. I needed everyone to be asleep so I could talk my way passed the authorities and show my credentials. You were having trouble falling asleep, so I helped you."

Everyone accepted that as they finished off their pastries and took their last sips of coffee.

Then Chen turned to Saleem. "In your prayer, did you call him Mr. Mike?"

"Yes, is that not his name?"

"Well, we don't know his full name. We just call him Big Mike."

"Why do you call him Big Mike?" Saleem wondered.

Everyone turned to Big Mike, his muscular arms bulging out of his uniform. Big Mike looked up from his phone. "What?"

Saleem nodded. "I get it."

Then Chen added. "What is your full name, Big Mike?"

"You wouldn't understand."

Josh thought that was a strange answer. "It's hard to pronounce?"

"You wouldn't understand what would happen to you if you knew my full name," he said with a chuckle.

Everyone sighed and deflated, backing off on the questioning.

Chen took the talk in another direction. "So, tour guide Hajj, what is Taba?"

Hajj wiped his mouth. "Taba is a border town right off the southernmost tip of Israel and the eastern most point of Egypt. It's a border crossing that's a resort town that has traded hands between countries.

It once belonged to Egypt then it became Israeli in 1989 when it was given back to Egypt. Now it's a resort town enjoyed by both Egyptians and Israelis."

Maria pointed to the water. "What body of water is that?"

The water was a beautiful blue with a cool 72-degree breeze blowing over it. The whole scene felt so inviting to Josh, like nature was calling him to dive in.

"The Gulf of Aqaba," Hajj continued. "The Sinai Peninsula is the eastern part of Egypt and two bodies of water define its eastern and western coastlines. The Gulf of Aqaba on the east and the Gulf of Suez on the west."

Josh was about to say "That's interesting" but Hajj pushed on.

"First Kings 9 says that King Solomon built ships at Ezion Geber, near Elath in Edom, which we passed, right Big Mike?"

"Right," he nodded.

"This was also a place where the Israelites camped in Numbers 33. It's very important in the Israelites adventures in this area."

Josh took a sip of coffee and asked, "Was that before or after the Red Sea thing?"

"After. Like twenty or thirty years after."

Josh replied. "Now, I don't know my Bible very well, but the Red Sea is what Moses walked over, right?"

Hajj found that funny. "Sort of. First, God told him to hold out his staff and then God split the Red Sea in half, creating dry land in the middle that they then walked through. Only Jesus would be the one to walk right over the water."

"Magnificent," Saleem sighed.

"Unbelievable," Josh added. Coming from him that word had a different meaning.

"You don't believe that happened?" Chen must have picked up on Josh's tone.

Everyone turned to Josh, putting him on the spot. "We've seen some pretty incredible things. A massive flood. Fireballs from the sky. But, c'mon, a sea opened up? Water doesn't split in two. That completely defies the properties of H2O." Nobody responded right away, leaving Josh hanging. "Right?"

"Hear, O Israel: The LORD our God, the LORD is one," Saleem said.

"What does that mean?"

"Any miracle you saw before came from the same God. If He was powerful before with Noah and Abraham, He can be powerful again with Moses. God created water. He made it rain, flooding the earth, and Jesus walked over water, so it seems He could split it in half if He wanted. Who are we to say how much God can and cannot do?"

Josh didn't like that Saleem schooled him, but Saleem's answer felt right. Better to just change subjects. "So where is this Red Sea?"

Hajj pointed to a place behind Josh. "Actually, it's right there."

Josh turned and looked at it again. Palm trees filled the shoreline and Josh immediately thought it looked like Florida which he had seen in ads …

In a flash the scene changed.

Josh stood on dry ground in the middle of something confusing. He couldn't understand what he was seeing. Wind blew mightily into his face. Water churned in stereo in both ears as two forty-foot walls of water stood one hundred feet across from each other, on his right and on his left.

Ahead of him, a mass of people crossed to one side. There must have been hundreds of thousands of men, women, and children, carrying their belongings in a hurry toward a shoreline, because, behind him, Josh could hear another rumbling, so he turned and saw an approaching enemy.

A hundred chariots charged into the water valley, racing toward the people mass. Their horses gave them the advantage of speed.

The people started to understand their predicament and started to murmur, cry, and scream.

Josh stood right in the middle of the two groups, his feet frozen in place. The chariots charged at him from one direction. The people were beginning to climb on to land by the hundreds. Josh pivoted back to the chariots, which had gotten so close he could see the chariot rider's faces—stern, focused, angry, and hard. It was Pharaoh's army.

All the chariots were now in the valley between the two walls of water, gaining quickly on the innocent runners. They had no defense against the wave of metal monsters descending on them.

Then, from the far shoreline inward, the water began to fall as the liquid walls disintegrated into the sea. Chariot after chariot was swallowed into the raging sea, taking out the last chariot to enter the danger zone and collapsing toward Josh and the terrified masses helping each other to the shoreline, then stopping to look back at the sea. They had an incredible view of it all.

So did Josh.

The first chariot drivers sensed the Red Sea closing in on them, snapping their reigns to make the horses go faster. Josh could tell their focus shifted from catching the people to getting out of the flood zone to save their lives. A wave sucked under them and roared toward Josh who …

Awoke to water splashing into his face.

Chen held the glass in his hand as Maria, Hajj, Chen, Saleem, and Big Mike looked down on him. Josh saw their concerned faces, then scurried on his back along the stone covered deck to escape the tidal wave that never came. He tripped over a chair that wrapped around his legs causing him to fall again.

Big Mike grabbed Josh and bear hugged him until Josh's mind realized where he was.

"What, what, what did you see? Josh!" Maria demanded.

Tourists around them stood and grabbed their stuff. Some left, not wanting to be around this chaos. It was their vacation and Josh was ruining their vibe.

Josh caught his breath. "The Red Sea."

The team jumped into the SUV and found a place in the parking lot to stop. They were creating too much attention at this little tourist spot and needed to separate. This gave Josh time to gather his thoughts. As soon as Big Mike put the vehicle into park, everyone turned to Josh who told them about the split sea, the people running for their lives and the army on chariots chasing them and eventually drowning horribly.

"Wow! You saw that last great moment when God closed the Red Sea around Pharaoh's chariots, completely wiping out his army," Hajj said. "Spectacular."

"And unusual. Three visions in twenty-four hours," Maria said. "That's a lot."

"Definitely," said Chen. "God is giving us plenty of clues. But this vision feels different. Your other visions were symbolic and prophetic, but with this one you were right in the middle of the actual scene."

Josh exhaled deeply. "I could feel it, not just see it."

Saleem rose his hand, not sure how this all worked. "So this vision you had, what caused it?"

Josh thought for a second. "When I turned, I saw the Red Sea. But that's not the Red Sea. Hajj, you said it was Aqaba."

"Technically it's a gulf that flows off the Red Sea. Aqaba is not mentioned in the Bible, but the Red Sea is mentioned like twenty-six times. So for the Israelites this was the Red Sea."

Chen raised his hand, his eyebrows furled. "Wait, are you saying the Israelites crossed the Red Sea here? How far is this from where the Israelites started?"

Hajj thought for a moment, "Like … 266 miles."

"Are you saying the Israelites crossed all that distance then crossed the Red Sea?" Chen's tone challenged Hajj who nodded his head before he spoke.

"Some archaeologists believe they crossed this way. Yes, it would have taken two or three weeks with all those people but listen to these stats. The Gulf of Suez is like 150 feet deep at its deepest. The Gulf of Aqaba is six thousand feet at its deepest. The scholars debate the magnitude of the miracle."

Chen laughed, "Whether it happened here or there, it's still pretty miraculous."

Hajj smiled, understanding clearly now. "Remember this is one of the most unbelievable, mind-blowing miracles of the Bible. So incredible, it's a story that people have been telling for over three thousand years. So was it a puddle or a deep, blue sea that God parted?"

Josh could tell that everyone understood Hajj's line of thought.

Saleem broke the silence. "So why did Josh get that vision now?"

Everybody stopped to ponder. Josh broke the silence. "I went from a darkness vision to a parting sea vision. Why?"

Maria jumped in. "Maybe the darkness vision is where we are heading, but the Red Sea is all about right now."

"What do we need to know about right now?" Big Mike sounded impatient.

Chen got it. "Chariots."

Hajj agreed. "Chariots."

Maria too. "Of course, that has to be it. Bales is looking for chariot parts as a time marker to go back to the time of Moses."

"Has anyone found chariot parts in these waters?" Josh wondered.

"These are deep waters," Hajj said. "I'm pretty sure some have tried. If Pharaoh's entire army of chariots got washed away, all that metal would sink fast. It could be a chariot junk yard down there."

"But that intense flood also could have stirred up a lot of sand and buried it all even deeper," Saleem added.

Hajj agreed. "And it's been over three thousand years."

"Does that mean Bales is going scuba diving?" Josh added. "These are tourist areas. There's probably a diving shop nearby."

Everyone piled out of the room and ran to the lobby. Chen asked the front desk clerk about scuba diving and was directed to Babu's Dive Shop on the water.

Racing but not trying to panic, the group pushed toward a shack on the water and a hand-painted sign that said something in Arabic then clearly something in English, "Babu's Dive Shop."

They quickly tried the door. It was locked. Hajj pounded on the door. "Hello, is anyone here?" No answer. Now what?

A man walked by. He looked like the quintessential beach bum. He wore a T-shirt with a Ford Mustang on it. His jeans were cut off and tattered. His flip flops had flopped more than they flipped. His face had a patchy beard, and his eyes were covered with reflective sunglasses.

"They're not in," he said. The man spoke like California surfer with a slight middle eastern accent.

"Do you know when they're coming back?" Chen pressed him.

The man shrugged and looked to the sky, maybe for an answer. "Hard to say."

This carefree man slowed things down too much. Chen took a breath for patience. "Do you know this Babu?"

"Oh, yeah. I know him."

"Could you maybe call him?"

The man giggled. "That would be weird."

"Why?" Chen asked.

"Because I would be calling myself!"

"Wait, you're Babu?" Hajj inquired.

"In the flesh."

"Why didn't you say that?" Chen breathed, calming himself.

"You didn't ask. You were talking about him in the third person so I just joined you."

Babu unlocked the wooden door to the dive shack. The door creaked as it opened. The musty smell of water hit their noses as Big Mike walked in first, doing a security check. All seemed good.

The walls were filled with pictures of Babu diving around sunken ships with all kinds of people. One of them looked like Tom Cruise, but Josh couldn't be sure.

Maria proceeded with the questioning. "We're looking for a man. This man." She pulled out the photo of Bales they had gotten in the reflection of the mirror before heading back to the time of Noah. Babu studied it carefully and calmly.

"I know that dude."

Everyone perked up. Big Mike whipped out his phone and started dialing, pressing buttons, texting.

"Was he here? When was he here?" Maria continued.

"Yesterday. Late."

"What was he asking about?"

"What every archaeologist asks about—the crossing of the Red Sea."

"What was he looking for?" Hajj pushed.

"Chariot wheels."

Suddenly it made sense to Josh. Chariot wheels need to be metal, sturdy, iron. The chariots were swallowed up by the collapsing walls of water but it would be the wheels which would stand the erosion of time. Of course. That's what Bales would be after.

"Are there any?" Josh said. "Have you seen them?"

"Naw. But I've been out there looking for them. When I was younger. Like two years ago. A doctor guy from America. Him." Babu pointed to a picture of himself and an older man with a safari hat, mid-60s, with a little belly, red splotchy hair and a long curly beard. "Dr. Conrad Turner. Have you heard of him?"

Nobody had, not even Hajj.

"He swears those chariots are out there. We dove together, looked and dug around a bunch. Saw nothing. Not sayin' they aren't there. Just haven't seen them myself and I've been all over those waters. But it's deep. Aqaba is over a mile deep in places."

Everyone took a breath to assess all this information they had just received. Maria took the opportunity during the pause and pointed to his clothes and said, "By the way, I like your shirt."

Babu seemed genuinely grateful. "Ah, thanks. Cool car."

"She has one like it," Josh added.

Babu went speechless, uttering a hushed "Whoa."

She continued, "But you haven't been down a mile deep in that sea."

"Yeah, that's true. We can only go like 200 feet. Even the doc gave up at 150."

"So what would you need to get down there?"

Babu thought for a second. "Like … a sub."

Outside they heard a sound and, right on cue, everyone spilled out the door and began running down the shore line, looking at the water. The reflecting sun made it hard to see clearly, but Josh saw him—Bales—on a jet ski heading out into the waters. "There! Over there!"

Big Mike somehow had binoculars on him, scanning the waters. "Confirmed." He handed the binoculars to Josh who found Bales. Bales stopped the jet ski, turning off the motor. He turned, knowing he was being watched, looking straight at Josh. That smile. Josh's breath caught.

"Bales."

Josh handed the binoculars to Babu who examined Bales. "Yep that's him. Is he a bad guy?"

"Oh yeah," was all Josh could say.

Then, behind Bales, the water began to gurgle as a tower emerged from the water. A submarine arrived, like an Uber, to take Bales under the sea. Bales climbed the ladder and entered the submarine through an open hatch. Once securely tightened, the sub submerged and Bales was gone.

"Is he in a submarine?" Chen cried. Josh nodded. "A sub? He got a sub? How does someone get a submarine?"

"Money talks," Hajj replied.

"Then get us a sub. Your parents have money."

"My parents could probably rent a sub, but you need to find one and transport it here. That takes time. Bales had this all planned."

Big Mike interrupted, hanging up his call and confirming their suspicions. "Yeah, getting a sub would take too much time. I would need five days which we don't have."

Something about seeing Bales' face and that smile set Josh off. He was livid. He wanted Bales stopped. Hurt. Dead! He wanted his dad back. Bales was all the evil in his life and more. "We have to get out there and stop him!" he screamed.

Josh's outburst scared everyone because of its intensity. Josh took a couple breaths while Maria leaned up next to him. "Remember, it's God who will avenge. He will repay. Our job is to make sure Bales doesn't get his hands on anything that will help him travel back in time."

Josh closed his eyes, nodding.

"But how are we going to get out there?" Chen asked.

Big Mike held up his phone. "I have a boat equipped with sonar on its way. But it will take six hours."

"Bales may grab what he needs and be gone by then," Saleem offered.

Suddenly a 30-foot boat roared toward them. The shape looked like a killer whale, with a round nose and single big glass eye. The body was white with a black head and black fins. Upon closer look,

Josh could see on the side it read, "Glass Bottom Boat Rentals" and it was moving pretty briskly. The driver slowed down the engines and drifted toward the coastline. The captain stepped out. It was Babu. "Anybody need a ride?"

9

Babu gunned the boat like a pro. The rest of the group surrounded the oval shaped glass bottom that peered into the sea. There were seats around the glass but nobody wanted to sit, busily trying to look into the water for some sign of life. It was all passing by too quickly.

"We use this for tourists. They love the design and you can see some pretty radical stuff—lionfish, turtles, frogfish, stonefish, even sharks and moray eels."

And maybe an evil villain trying to destroy the world, Josh hoped.

Babu took the boat to the approximate area where Bales descended into the sub. Everyone leaned on the safety railings. Josh wasn't sure if the glass would hold if he fell forward, and he didn't want to find out. Slowly Babu shifted the engine to a putt-putt-putt across the surface. While everyone looked down. They could see some rocks and vegetation then the further they went out into the water, the view turned dark, except for a few fish.

For a couple of hours, nobody really said anything, except an occasional "look at that" or "check this out" but they were completely focused on catching a glimpse of Bales and the sub.

Big Mike looked concerned checking his phone repeatedly.

During a lull when things seemed hopeless, Josh wandered up to Babu at the controls. "Thanks again for helping us out."

"No problem, bro. You guys sounded pretty desperate. I don't know what this guy did but it doesn't sound nice."

"Well, he kidnapped my dad and killed my mom."

Babu stumbled backwards. "Whoa! That's intense! No wonder you want him eliminated."

Josh looked over at Maria who smiled back. "Well, we'll see about that."

"But I got to ask, what do you want with the chariot wheel, except maybe a nice museum piece?"

Josh tried to imagine where to start with this. His pause took a long awkward time.

Babu waved it off. "It's cool, no problem. Sounds like it would blow my mind."

"It would definitely do that. So are you into this whole Bible thing? You said you came out here with doctor or archaeologist."

"Oh, yeah, Dr. Samuels? He was an interesting dude, but, I don't know. I've seen some strange things out here. I couldn't say for sure there's no God and I can't say for sure there is."

"This place is where some believe Moses crossed the sea?"

Babu exhaled, shaking his head. "Yeah, that would be a sight. I guess if I saw that I would believe."

Josh smiled, then wondered …

Why don't I believe? I've seen it. Kinda.

Josh did see it in his vision, experienced it, could feel the wind, and taste the sea water. It was about as real as he could imagine. Still he held back.

The glass bottom boat got repetitious and they were running out of gas soon. As if on cue, Big Mike's crew pulled up in a 230-foot yacht, three decks with a helicopter pad on the front.

"Big Mike!" Josh cried. "How in the world?"

The team joined Josh in awe, pressing Big Mike for an answer as to how he got such a huge, well-stocked boat.

All he said was, "It helps to know people. But I wish it were a sub. Let's go."

Babu shook his head. "Can't compete with that." Maria hugged him as the others gathered to thank Babu.

"Dude," Chen said, "You were exactly who we needed when we needed someone. You really saved us."

The rest of the team said their goodbyes then jumped aboard Big Mike's battleship.

Big Mike held out a card to Babu. "Here's my number if anything comes up."

Babu read the card and showed the others. "Simplest business I've ever seen." It was a white card with black letters that read "Mike" with his phone number.

A man of few words … even on his business card!

Babu waved as they pulled away. He kind of looked sad saying goodbye to his new friends; however, Josh and the others refocused on their new ride. This yacht had all the perks. Five other soldiers quietly worked the bottom deck filled with radar equipment. One of them steered drones that took off from the deck and scanned the waters and coastline. Josh watched as the man operated the joysticks. He felt, after only a couple minutes, that he could work those, just as he steered his dad's mechanical spy mouse.

On board the ship, there was even a kitchen with snacks and sandwiches. Big Mike thinks of everything. Josh helped himself to some.

Maria and Saleem sat in the back on a couch overlooking the beautiful sunset. Josh had to force himself to take his eyes off them and on to the beautiful sky. It was a nice farewell to the strenuous day.

Chen and Hajj watched over the shoulders of Big Mike's crew, who worked diligently and without a word to each other.

Big Mike crossed over and gave the team an update. "No sign of him. Our sonar goes down about 200 feet and this body of water is like a mile long. We have ears listening for submarine sound waves, but they know how to fool ships on the surface. We have two drones with infrared scanning the coastline also."

Chen scratched his head. "Didn't Babu say he and this archaeologist guy looked for artifacts and didn't find anything?"

Hajj replied, "Yeah but they were diving in suits and could only go down like 100–150 feet. That submarine can go much further, like 1,500 feet. Some specialized subs can go down like 4,000 feet."

"Wait a minute," Josh interrupted. "If you are saying this is where the Israelites crossed, how could it be like a mile deep?"

"That's a good question, Josh." Hajj took a moment to think or receive information, however it was that he knew so much. "There's a lot of speculation about which body of water they crossed. The Old Testament, written in Hebrew, used the words *Yam Suph* to name the body of water. Yam means *sea* and Suph means *reeds*. Reeds grow in a shallow body of water. But your vision didn't look like a shallow body of water?"

Josh agreed. "No, it was deep, but not a mile."

"Right. Reeds are like the marshland where Moses floated in his little boat as a baby. So there's another use of the word *suph* which means *end*. *Yam Suph* could mean *Sea at the End*. The sea at the end of Egypt. Right over there ..." Hajj pointed to the land to the west. "... that's Egypt. Over on the other side ... is not Egypt. Most likely Midian in Moses' day."

"Very interesting. But my vision had Israelites crossing maybe 100 feet down, not a mile."

Hajj motioned to the area behind them. "Right over there, back toward Babu's shack, the water is shallow, like one hundred or one hundred fifty feet deep. That's most likely where it occurred and why you had that vision there. Kind of like when Chen heard those voices around the Tower of Babel. But scientists have scanned that area and found nothing. It was 3,500 years ago, sands shift, water currents move. The chariots may be deeper down and that sub gives him an advantage."

"We can't match them with our equipment right now. We'll patiently wait," Big Mike said. "They have to come out some time."

"Where do you think they'll come out?" Josh wondered.

Big Mike pulled out a map of the peninsula and the two finger gulfs, the Gulf of Suez and the Gulf of Aqaba. "If he finds the chariot, then he'll need to time travel here, where the Nile delta is."

"The land of Goshen where the Israelites lived," Hajj further explained.

"Correct. That means Bales would want to travel up the Suez to get the closest to his target area. We're going to wrap around the southern tip, entering the Red Sea and keep looking for him in this direction."

"As long as he finds his chariot artifact," Saleem emphasized.

Big Mike agreed. "Yes, it's a long shot that he could find something in this short amount of time that archaeologists have been looking for over decades."

That seemed good to everyone, except Josh, who held his opinion. Maria watched him and Josh knew she knew so he decided to just express it once everyone dispersed.

"It's going to take too long. It's giving Bales too much room to operate."

"What else can we do," Maria asked.

Josh had no answer.

Saleem, sitting next to Maria, chimed in. "We have to be strong and courageous. Do not be afraid or terrified because of them, for the LORD your God goes with us; he will never leave us nor forsake us."

Josh wasn't getting any support here so he slipped off to the front of the luxury cruiser and took in the cool air. Slowly he fell asleep.

Hours later, as morning dawned, Josh shot up, awake, looking around at his surroundings. The coast line look similar but they were in a different place. He saw Big Mike with his binoculars scanning the coastline.

"Any luck?"

Big Mike dropped the binoculars from his eyes. "No."

"Where are we?"

"We're in the Gulf of Suez."

"Isn't it shallow here?"

"Very shallow. Like 200 feet. We've flown drones over this area. He's not here."

Josh could see the large oil tankers lumbering in and out of the gulf. "Amazing those ships can slip through."

Hajj, who seemed to sense when information was needed, walked up. "Yeah, those big ships are wide and long but not deep. They can pass through 70-foot waters."

"Big Mike, are you sure Bales didn't come out anywhere around here?"

"Positive. We have drones, satellites, and the radar from this vessel searching everything over here. We've covered about one hundred miles of coastline tonight."

"The Sinai Peninsula is pretty huge. Two hundred forty miles from north to south and one hundred thirty miles from …" Hajj paused, at a loss for words. "From …"

"Hajj, are you okay?" Josh asked.

"I can't remember. Wow."

"Did you get any sleep?"

"Not much."

"You're just tired. Maybe a nap would help."

Big Mike's phone rang. He quickly answered it. "Hello?" After a second, he put the phone on speaker.

The unmistakable Babu's voice rang out. "Dudes, who's there listening?"

"I'm here," said Josh. "And Hajj. What's up?" As Babu continued, Maria, Saleem, and Chen slowly gathered, coming up from the lower decks.

"I'm sending a picture from a security camera from a friends' paddleboard business in Taba. He saw this submarine in the water and a guy coming out of it."

Big Mike's phone dinged and Mike checked his messages. Big Mike studied it, concerned. "Oh, yeah."

Everyone perked up, wanting to the see the picture. As he showed it to the group, everyone understood.

"That's your guy, right?" Babu asked.

Josh realized at that moment that Bales returned to where he started while they searched for where they thought he was going. Josh stomped his feet and punched the air.

Maria studied the photo closely. The photo was shadowy but definitely Bales. And he was carrying something covered with a canvas or tarp. "What is that in his hand?"

Chen looked. "Could be a chariot wheel or maybe the time machine."

Everyone realized what Chen just said and who was listening.

Babu replied on the phone, sounding very confused. "Uh, did you just say … time machine?"

Chen was quick on his feet. "Yeah, what I meant was that it's a machine that estimates the time frame that the object came from. Used in archaeology for dating relics." Chen shrugged at the others who responded by making faces that silently said "sounds good" or "yeah, kinda."

Babu seemed to process that and said, "Okay, sure. I mean a real time machine, huh, that would be hard to believe for sure."

Everyone replied this time, saying "Totally." "Yeah, no way." "That's crazy."

Babu acted satisfied. "Okay, well I hope that helped."

"Babu, thank you so much. You are amazing," Josh said.

"Yeah, I hope you get your dad back, Josh."

"Thanks Babu. 'Bye."

Big Mike hung up. Minutes later, the ship docked at a tiny port and the team got out where a brand new SUV greeted them.

They were at a crossroads now and all signs confirmed that they had unfortunately lost Bales' trail.

10

Big Mike pulled out his map and set it on the hood. Everyone surrounded the map.

Chen spoke up first. "What are we going to do?"

Big Mike pointed to places on the map. "If Bales has the chariot wheel, then he's heading here, to the area known back then as Goshen. It's west of Port Said and Port Ismailia along the Suez Canal, the area known as the Nile Delta. If he didn't get the chariot wheel, then he's still on the hunt for a time marker. That means he's going either here, Saint Catherine's Monastery which some believe was Mount Sinai where Moses got the Ten Commandments or into Cairo which is full of all kinds of relics, especially the Museum in Cairo."

"Do you think there's anything in either place?" Josh asked.

Hajj spoke up. He seemed himself after his little brain pop. "As far as I know, nobody has ever found any relics of Moses and the Israelites."

Chen tapped his head, hoping to rattle off some information stuck in there. "Didn't God tell Moses to chisel out two stone tablets like the first ones and come up to him on the mountain. And also to make a wooden ark covered in gold? Seems like there would something to find."

Hajj sighed. "All of those things, the stone tablets and the ark of the covenant made it to Jerusalem by the time of David. They are not here."

"So where should we go?" Maria asked. The silence was awkward.

Josh remembered when his mom showed him a movie at Easter called *The Ten Commandments*. "That's the mountain Moses climbed and like talked to God or something?"

"Yeah, Mount Sinai," Chen answered.

"So where is that from where we are now?"

"Well, it's a lot of places. Somewhere around thirteen locations have been suggested as the real Mount Sinai," Hajj said. "Sure, it's an important place because it's where Moses met God and received the Ten Commandments so that means pilgrims want to travel to it and pay their respects, but it's just that—a tourist trap."

"Is there any place," Josh probed deeper, "that has some history to it where some piece of archaeology could be found?"

Big Mike pointed to a spot on the map. "Our best bet is Jebel Musa, or The Mountain of Moses, which is right where Saint Catherine's Monastery is located. It's over 7,000 feet above sea level. It's in the southern part of the Sinai Peninsula, where we are right now."

Josh sat up, now excited. "How far is that from us?"

Big Mike was already searching for the answer on his phone. "Two and a half hours from here by car."

"We should go!" Josh waited for confirmation. The group stirred sensing controversy. Maria made a semi-courtesy face with a little shrug added.

Hajj vehemently shook his head. "I don't think we'll find anything. It's a dead end. A museum of art, not artifacts."

"I've always been curious," Chen admitted.

"Let's go!" Josh announced.

"Have you had a vision about Mount Sinai?" Hajj countered. "We usually follow your visions before we take a next step."

"No, but we have no other direction so why not just check it out?"

Hajj protested further. "Guys, I'm telling you. The artifacts at Jebel Musa are from the wrong centuries."

"C'mon, we're here. Why not?" Chen asked.

"I didn't know we were here to sightsee," Hajj gritted, growing angrier in his response. "I thought we were trying to find some guy who wanted to end the world."

"Hey, if we're curious, maybe Bales is too. We'll cut him off there." Josh felt good about the decision and Maria seemed okay too.

"Fine!" Hajj pouted and slammed the car door shut as he got in the vehicle.

The others gave the curious what's-up-with-him glances then got into their usual spots. Big Mike punched the coordinates into his GPS and they were off.

Josh looked at the directions. As a bird flew, the mountain was near their location, but there was one problem. A giant mountain chain was in their way. They would have to go around.

Saleem, ever curious, read from his phone. "St. Catherine's Monastery was built in AD 530. There's a Christian church there and an Islamic mosque. But there's also a library with lots of ancient texts."

"I'm assuming no writings from Moses?" Josh asked.

Hajj leaned forward from the back seat. "The only writing he did happened on a rock. We don't have the actual Ten Commandments etched on stone. As I've said, there are no known archaeological evidences of Moses and the Israelites from that time."

"Why not?" Saleem surprisingly asked (what Josh was thinking).

"These people were part of a poor shepherd community. They didn't leave behind anything. The Bible says God even kept their clothes and shoes from wearing out so they didn't discard much. Food came from heaven in the form of manna so they didn't cultivate or plant. They were nomads who lived in tents and packed up to move to the next destination. Plus this was 3,400 years ago. Things just don't survive for that long." Hajj leaned back, looking disheartened. "As I said, I don't feel confident about this, but, why not, we're right here."

Josh wished Hajj didn't pout so much but he was an eight-year-old with the brain of a fifty-year-old college professor. It had to be hard to balance the two emotions inside him.

The conversation remained silent for nearly two hours of the trip while people slept. Saleem broke the silence as they were thirty minutes outside of their destination by reading Exodus 19 as the Israelites approached Mount Sinai, just as they were doing, except in an air-conditioned vehicle. Chen prayed. Josh felt it comforted the others, except Hajj who just looked out the window.

The vehicle climbed the increasing elevations along the highway, but during this last part the climb steepened. Signs now started to point to St. Catherine's Monastery.

Everyone was awake and alert as they entered the dirt parking lot. This wasn't a tourist destination like Universal Studios with sharply manicured attendants pointing the way, but more like dropping into a flea market. Josh remembered the cheesy destinations along the American interstates that boasted strange monstrous zoos with two-headed alligators. This had that same unkept appearance.

However, even Josh could feel the sanctity of this moment. Something about this place felt … respectful … despite the outward appearance of the drive-in parking lot.

The monastery was a walk from the car. Buildings, chapels, and religious icons popped up over the dirt-covered walls that surrounded the place. It looked like a fort. What was it keeping out? Or in?

Big Mike paid who he needed to pay and the group entered. Josh remembered bits and pieces of the story, again mostly from the film. There was a Chapel of the Holy Bush where God first talked to Moses.

Saleem looked around. "I don't see any remanent of a bush here?"

They saw the Chapel of the Well where Moses met his future wife. Conveniently these were all within easy walking distance.

Hajj walked around just shaking his head. "These things didn't all happen here. I'm telling you we won't find anything in this place. No bush. No well. No Ten Commandments."

"Just coffee," Chen said, drinking a tiny cup he had just purchased from a vendor. "Did Moses drink coffee? Because this is good!" Now everyone wanted one in addition to assorted bags of nuts and candies. This "monastery" had a tourist shop with snacks and knick-knacks.

Chen talked to those who looked monk-ish about the contents inside the monastery, trying not to raise any suspicion. But the consensus was—no original artifacts could be found. Chen whispered to Josh, "I don't want to tell Hajj he was right, but he was right. He's just being so weird about it."

Everyone comfortably visited their own sections of the monastery. Maria seemed most interested in the artwork and mosaics in the chapels.

Saleem perused the ancient Bible manuscripts in glass cases. Even Josh admitted they were beautiful.

Hajj examined the oldest library in the world that smelled musty and smart.

Josh found himself staring at something the museum called the Christ Pantocrator. It was a painting of Jesus holding what looked like a Bible and what two fingers raised, like a limp peace sign.

"I promise you Jesus didn't have a Bible like that," Maria quietly whispered. The place had a library sacredness to it. "The Bible said He was the Word of God and that's what the artist wanted to express."

"I feel like I've seen this before?" Josh said.

Maria read the inscription. "It's one of the most iconic pictures in this whole monastery. It dates back to the sixth century. Jesus is called a Pantocrator which means ruler of all."

Josh couldn't shake the fact that he had seen this or had seen someone who looked like this. The Shepherd? Josh felt a wave of deja vu at this moment.

Big Mike walked in. Hajj followed him. "Big Mike, we're not going to find anything in here. No artifacts taking us back 3,000 years. We're just wasting our time."

"I know," he gently replied. "But it's always good to cover all our bases and make sure. It's possible Bales could come here, and that's what is most important."

Hajj shook his head. "The oldest thing in here is the Codex Sinaiticus. It's the oldest Greek manuscript in the world, but it only dates back to the fourth century AD. There's even a treaty signed by the Prophet Muhammad telling people not to raid this monastery and loot it. Everything else is sixth century AD."

"I understand," Big Mike said firmly, appearing to be annoyed by Hajj's reaction. Josh never liked seeing Big Mike mad.

Hajj wanted an explanation but didn't get it. He stormed out. Hajj looked mad, madder than Josh had ever seen him. Josh and Maria exchanged looks wondering what was up.

Josh pointed at something in the display case. "Oh, I found the Ten Commandments." Josh walked out, leaving Maria and Big Mike wondering what he meant. It was a book sized painting of the Ten Commandments, hardly the real thing.

Outside, Josh found Hajj looking at the mountains.

"You okay?" Josh asked.

"No."

"Care to elaborate?"

Hajj took a moment then went off. "I've been given this gift for a reason but nobody listens to me. I knew this place was a waste of time but here we are, stumbling around like tourists. I thought we were after a bad guy who wants to destroy the world. Am I the only one who cares?"

"Well, that bad guy killed my mom and kidnapped my dad who could be dead. So I care."

Hajj looked like he knew he had messed up. Josh figured Hajj didn't have the maturity to apologize. "Whatever" was all he could say and walked to the car. The others started to gather there also.

Josh took one final look at the mountain before him, the sun setting over it. The sign in front of him pointed right at it, saying

"Mount Sinai." The mountain where Moses received the Ten Commandments? Maybe. Certainly an impressive view.

Everyone sat in silence as Big Mike drove. Hajj's mood cast a gloom over their trip west.

A few dozen minutes into the trip, Maria broke the silence. "What now?"

There was a pause, mostly in hopes that Hajj would jump in. He just stared out the window.

Saleem offered a suggestion. "What about the Pharaoh of that time? Who was it?"

Nobody could answer. Chen turned to Hajj. "Hajj, this is your moment to shine."

Hajj huffed. "Most believe it was Ramses II. He was king of Egypt from 1279 to 1213 BC. He built a lot of stuff and had a ton of children."

"How many?" Josh had to ask.

"Like one hundred." Everyone groaned at the thought.

"Any artifacts or maybe … some trinkets?" Maria asked.

Hajj thought for a moment, maybe another dramatic pause. "There's a huge statue of him at the Egyptian Museum in Cairo and his mummy."

Chen nearly ejected out of the roof. "His mummy! Why didn't you say anything!"

Hajj shrugged. "You didn't ask. You wanted to run around this old mountain."

"Just like Bales did with Abraham, maybe he's after Ramses' DNA," Maria reminded Hajj, who grimaced at the thought.

Hajj gagged. "Uh, don't remind me of that."

Big Mike was already punching coordinates into his phone. "There's an airport close by here called El Tor. It can get us to Cairo in minutes. I already have a plane en route."

Chen waved him off. "Hajj will fly the plane, don't worry." Again Hajj grimaced, the memory of flying—and crashing—that huge plane in Turkey still felt a little too raw and not something he wanted to repeat.

Josh caught Big Mike's attention. "We need a small airport to land. Too many people are looking for us at the big airports."

Big Mike was steps ahead of them. "Capital International Airport, east of Cairo, small and out of the way. It's ideal for us. We won't be bothered there."

He gunned the car's motor. Everyone could feel they were getting closer to their destiny.

11

The El Tor airport was exactly what the team needed—small and inconsequential. They saw no one as they boarded the private jet. Forty-five minutes later they landed at the Capital International airport, another unassuming airstrip that handled a small number of international flights.

Compared to the conflict they were used to at past airports, today's flight was a breeze. Another SUV with tinted windows met them by the plane. Big Mike drove them into Cairo.

Highway 50 stretched east to west, from Cairo to Taba and would be the most possible route Bales would take if he was driving. Big Mike let them know that his people were using satellite imaging to track any vehicles crossing this lonely stretch of dusty highway. So far, nothing suspicious had come up.

As they arrived in Cairo, Josh was convinced Cairo meant "chaos." The roads were jammed with cars that had horns that were apparently stuck on honking as long as the engine was running. Windows were rolled down, not for air conditioning but for cursing, so the driver could quickly and easily communicate his displeasure of the other drivers' skills. Chen winced many times and claimed he learned new words especially from the cab drivers.

Strangely, Hajj sat in the back just looking out the window. He was surprisingly quiet again, not like himself. Something about St. Catherine's sent him down a dark hole.

Instead, Saleem helped to pass the time by looking up stuff on his phone. "Did you know Cairo is the capital of Egypt and the name means the *victorious* after it was established when the Fatimids invaded it in AD 969 in a conquest for domination. They were victorious. Cairo is also the largest city in Africa with over 21 million people, the sixth largest in the world."

"And they are all driving right now," Chen joked. Everyone agreed.

"There are many great places to visit, such as the Pyramids of Giza and the Sphinx."

Everyone sat up. "I would love to see those," Saleem offered, saying exactly what Josh wanted to say. All eyes turned to Big Mike.

"In time," was all Big Mike said.

Time ... when we have time.

"Weren't those built by the Israelites? That's what I heard," Chen asked.

Saleem searched. "Hmmm, I'm not sure."

"No, the Jews were north of here in Goshen. Pharaoh Khufu built the ones in Egypt around 2550 BC and it was Egyptians who built it. The Jews built other things like a thousand years later. The Sphinx was built in 2500 BC by Pharaoh Khafre," Hajj replied.

"That's very interesting, Hajj," Maria said, trying to encourage him.

"I'm sure you could find all that on the internet," Hajj shrugged.

Maria looked like she wanted to respond, but Josh looked ahead and thought he saw it. "Wait, there's a river. Is that ... ?"

Everyone slid forward to see. A river flowed through the center of Cairo.

"Yep," Josh said. "The Nile."

Big Mike took a left before crossing it and pulled into a parking lot. While the group craned their necks to see the Nile, Big Mike parked and told them to head inside the big building across the street. A museum.

"Wait," Maria realized. "Where are we going?"

"The Egyptian Museum, also known as the Museum of Antiquities," Big Mike said. "Isn't that right, Hajj? This is where you told us
to go."

"Yep," Hajj replied, slipping out of his seat. "This is the place."

The building was three stories high, long, painted a pinkish hew,
with grandiose architecture. The structure itself was a work of art.
They just walked right in without any issue or questioning. Not even
a fee.

Inside however, was much different than the ornate outside. Josh
had been in the Smithsonian and the American Museum of Natural
History so he knew what a museum should look like.

This looked like someone's basement—an organizational
nightmare.

Some ancient stones and artifacts sat in glass cubes with red
velvet ropes attempting to keep people ten inches away, but other
things were just laying out—vases, bronze utensils, ancient stones
with carvings on them. There were some description cards so people
could know what this or that was, but not everything.

"When does the garage sale start?" Chen joked.

Josh looked around. "I don't see any guards either. Is security
based on the honor system?"

As they strolled through, Hajj explained. "I don't expect there to
be anything here of Jewish descent. Egyptians aren't really interested
in promoting that time period nor those people."

"And what would they find from that time period?" Saleem
asked.

"Good question Saleem. The Jews were slaves, very poor. This
was not their home so they did not have a lot of stuff, artifacts, works
of art. If Bales was here, he would be looking for things targeting
Ramses II."

"So we're to look for things that say Ramses II on it," Chen was
already off down the stairs.

"Yeah, and feel free to just grab it before Bales comes in and goes shopping," Josh concluded as he turned left.

But something was off about this location. Nobody could quite put their finger on it. It looked like someone had gone through here and looted. Josh remembered the riots in Egypt a while back where some museums in Egypt were targeted, but it was hard to imagine it was this bad.

Finally they found a construction worker and Hajj communicated with him (for once Chen wasn't needed for translation).

Chen looked lost. "It's not here."

"What's not here?" Hajj pressed.

"The museum. It moved. A new museum, called the Grand Egyptian Museum, was opened near the pyramids of Giza and all of the major artifacts have already been relocated."

"We're going to the pyramids!" Maria cried. The group let out a celebratory gasp. They would get to see the pyramids after all!

Everyone ran to the SUV, except Hajj who looked like he was in shock. While nobody voiced any concern, Josh understood what was bothering Hajj.

He was wrong.

As long as Josh had known him, Hajj had never got a fact wrong. It was his gift of knowledge and so far it had been perfect. Josh wondered how he didn't know the museum had moved. Something was wrong.

Hajj slumped into the van, closed the door, and they were off.

Big Mike crossed the Nile as everyone took in another huge look at the world's most famous river.

"Isn't the Nile the longest river in the world?" Saleem asked.

Maria replied, "Some say the Amazon in South America is longer. I remember a question in a history class final that said it was over 6,000 miles long! Isn't that right, Hajj?"

Hajj looked at the floor. He nodded. Maria glanced at Josh. She sensed it too. Maybe by throwing a softball question at him would increase his confidence. He said nothing.

"The amazing thing is that it flows north. All the other rivers flow south, but the Nile flows the opposite direction, from Africa to the Mediterranean. How does it do that, Hajj?" Chen asked. He too was trying to give Hajj an opportunity to shine.

Hajj shrugged. His moping diminished their excitement to learn more about the Nile. Even Big Mike looked in the rearview mirror to see what was up with him.

Josh turned to Hajj. "You okay?" Hajj nodded but it was clear he wasn't. Everyone gave him some emotional space.

Their view of the Nile ended quickly as they entered severe traffic, pushing west across Cairo, starting with a route straight down the middle of Cairo University. A number of mosques along the route declared calls to prayer, meaning it was 5 p.m. Hajj tensed up, that sound bringing up memories of forced prayer to an "Allah" he didn't believe in.

Josh turned again to ask Hajj if he was okay.

Hajj stalled for a moment before answering. "Yeah."

"Is the call to prayer bothering you?"

"Not really."

Maria leaned over, "What is it? Something is definitely bothering you. Is it because you got some information wrong?"

"How did I not know about the new museum? I know it's new information but the planning of it had to have been going on a long time. I don't even know any information about it, nothing is coming to mind. I just know the old stuff from the Cairo Museum."

"How can you read minds? I bet the website isn't even updated," Josh replied.

"I don't get my information from a website. It comes from God! Something's off. I feel it." Hajj dropped his head, looking like he was about to cry. "I let you guys down." Chen put an arm on his shoulder.

After a moment of silence, Saleem chimed in. "I haven't been doing this as long as you guys, but I imagine you are all very tired. Our spirits tire. David in the Psalms asked God to renew or refresh his spirit. If he asked to refresh that means his spirit was stale."

Everyone took in that wisdom. Josh wondered if a greater enemy they may face in the future is themselves.

"That's scary." Josh turned to Maria who again seemed only to be talking to him. "What would happen if you stopped getting visions or Chen stopped being able to translate."

Josh tried to take that idea in. "How do we keep that from happening?"

Maria continued. "Well, we're dealing with the spirit and the Bible makes it clear that our spirits hunger for manna."

"Manna?" Josh questioned. "What is that?"

Maria smiled. "It's the bread from heaven, God's word. Man does not live on bread alone but on every word that comes from the mouth of the Lord. Jesus quoted that while talking to the devil who was trying to tempt him."

Chen jumped in "We have to keep our spirits fresh through a biblical workout. We can't just expect this ability to be strong in us."

Josh was more confused than ever. First of all he didn't ask for this gift. He never read the Bible in his life. What he knew was quoted to him by his mom two years ago and now in the past few months he's been getting a crash course in Bible history.

"Yes, we can't forget that. We must fill up our own spiritual tanks," Maria said.

Chen recited a scripture from memory out loud, he said it slowly and methodically allowing everyone to drink it in. Saleem sighed when Chen finished. "Psalm 23 is one of my favorites."

As everyone enjoyed the Bible verses, Josh looked out the window. He saw road signs indicating that they were on Ring Road, an interstate, 75, that looked like a parking lot at times. Eventually the landscape began to open up, more desert and more browns. Definitely something he was familiar with in Las Vegas.

Then they appeared on the horizon. The three pyramids from a distance looked much smaller in person than in all the pictures they had seen, but as the road wound closer their immensity grew with their proximity. They looked like Legos at first glance and slowly grew to mountains. The road curved away from the pyramids, pointing them to a new man-made phenomena—the Grand Egyptian Museum.

Josh thought the Egyptian Museum in Cairo looked amazing on the outside but this was a man-made wonder. The gold reflective exterior wall designed with pyramids inside of pyramids stood nearly three stories tall. Josh actually skipped a breath.

They parked and walked toward the museum, feeling smaller with every step.

"Are they open?" Chen asked.

The parking lot had cars and it seemed active, but Josh wondered if they were coming or going.

They got to the ticket office and Chen communicated with them. He returned with news.

"They are closing at 6:00 p.m., in thirty minutes, and she's saying it's no use to come in. I said we will gladly buy a ticket for only thirty minutes to such a magnificent temple to Ra. They seemed to enjoy that."

Big Mike passed Egyptian pounds to Chen who passed them on and received the tickets. Immediately everyone ran in. Hajj walked slowly behind them all.

The insides were even more exhilarating than the outside. The three-story high ceiling populated by thirty- to fifty-foot-high statues caused everyone's hurry to pause. They had limited time to find Ramses II but they did not imagine such incredible architecture. They took it all in.

Chen found a worker and asked a question. The man pointed to the second floor and Chen waved everyone on. The signs thankfully were also in English in hopes of drawing an affluent English-speaking crowd so Josh knew they were heading to the Pharaohs and something called the Nineteenth Dynasty.

Hajj was unusually quiet and it made things awkward. Every time they went somewhere he usually couldn't stop talking about every little fact and figure. Now he just followed silently.

Finally they found the man they were looking for—Ramses II. Ramses' mummy lay in his giant sarcophagus. He looked scared and sunburnt, like a toasty brown. This was no mannequin. This was the dead man himself.

"Wow, that's him," Maria said. "That man right there talked to Moses."

"Check and see if he has a hard heart," Chen laughed.

"He wouldn't have any organs," Saleem replied. "They remove them all when they turn him into a mummy." Saleem missed the joke. Chen grimaced rolling his eyes.

Thankfully the mummy was in a glass case, a barrier to Bales' intentions. Big Mike ran his eyes all over it.

"Security system?" Josh asked.

"Hmm. It's hard to say. Things here are a little disconnected. They have all the parts they need for an amazing security system but I don't know if it all works. See that camera to your left?" The group looked up. "There should be a red light on just like the one over my head."

"Then again, when did Bales care about security systems or being seen?" Chen said.

Big Mike nodded. "True."

"What should we do," Maria asked. "Do we leave and come back tomorrow? Do we sit outside and monitor the activity? Or maybe we hide somewhere inside and sleep here?"

The group looked at Maria, surprised by what she had just said.

"When did you get so ambitious?" Josh replied. "You want to break the law?"

"It's for a greater cause. I've been paying attention," Maria smiled…deviously.

A voice came over the loud speaker announcing the museum's closing in ten minutes. It stated the message in French, Arabic and English.

"We don't even know if he's here or if he's coming," Saleem offered. "He could have a chariot wheel and headed to Goshen."

Everyone thought about all these options then looked to Josh, who responded, "What?"

"No visions?" Chen asked.

"If I had a vision, I'd be passed out on the ground right now! You'll know."

"Good point."

Josh scratched his head. "What if I'm too tired and not spiritually filled, like Saleem was saying. What do we do then?"

Big Mike zipped open a fanny pack and pulled out an interesting contraption, about two inches long and wide. He seemed to have a lens on it.

"What are you doing?" Josh asked Big Mike.

Big Mike did not reply, going to work and using his body to block any view. After fiddling with something, he turned without the contraption in his hands. Josh looked and saw the device attached, somehow, to an idol or a statute of some sort sitting nearby.

"It's a camera and it'll keep us updated 24/7. It's motion sensitive and will turn on when anyone moves in this area."

"Where are we going?" Saleem asked.

"Let's get some sleep," Big Mike answered. "We're obviously all tired. We traveled a lot today and we need to rest our bodies and our spirits. We have eyes everywhere until we figure out our next move."

12

Again, Hajj's parents' credit card proved another luxurious ben-efit. Everyone received a king-sized bedroom with a balcony looking right at the pyramids at a five-star hotel. Despite having Wi-Fi and giant flat screens in every room, Josh sat on the balcony all night watching the stars emerge from the darkness of the night, as the nearly full moon illuminated the pyramids. Josh couldn't imagine being anywhere else right now. A dream come true.

Only a stupid vision and a swan dive into the pool could ruin this night. But thankfully that didn't happen ...

That could only mean one thing—they were on the right track. The visions, he felt, course corrected their adventures and gave them clues when to pay attention.

Josh fell asleep on the balcony then woke up freezing during the night and slipped into bed. The next morning, after a delicious break-fast buffet, they loaded up their vehicle and set out toward northern Egypt.

Big Mike reported that Ramses' body remained untouched all night and nothing had been disturbed at the Grand Egyptian Museum. Big Mike steered them northeast along Ring Road.

In the car, there was light talk about what they had seen. Saleem led a devotional to get them started, reading a passage that said, "And now, Israel, what does the LORD your God ask of you but to fear the LORD your God, to walk in obedience to him, to love him, to serve the LORD your God with all your heart and with all your soul, and to observe the LORD's commands and decrees that I am giving you today for your own good?"

He spoke about the biblical understanding of "fear," which Josh always found confusing.

Josh noticed how quiet Hajj was throughout the talk, unusual for him to not point out the Hebrew meaning of words or locations that they passed. Finally, Chen spoke up, also noticing it.

"Hajj, buddy, you okay? I'm missing all the obscure trivia I could one day use on *Jeopardy*."

"I got nothing. You can look stuff up on Wikipedia if you're interested."

"But it's not the same unless I hear it from you."

"I think God is done with me. He's done speaking through me."

Everyone, but Josh, vocally protested. Josh understood Hajj's sentiment and believed he too could lose his ability anytime, on a whim.

Saleem leaned into Hajj. "Hajj, I've only known you a short amount of time, but I don't think any of this could have gone this far without you. You've been in more scary situations than anyone. It's okay for you to doubt. God only pulls back His hand and allows you distress so you will come running back to Him. We see that in the Exodus story over and over. Use this depression as a push into revelation."

Chen chimed in also. "You know, buddy, you remind me of Solomon. He was the smartest guy ever in the Old Testament. He struggled having all that knowledge too. Wrote a whole book about it—Ecclesiastes."

Hajj showed some life in his eyes. He nodded, accepting the encouragement, while not yet seeming to fully believe it.

"Do we have any clue as to where we're going?" Maria asked Big Mike.

Suddenly Big Mike slammed on the brakes of the car. Everyone froze. Quite an extreme reaction to a simple question. Behind them they could hear the screeching of tires and curses from the drivers. Big Mike listened to a voice in his ear, his earpiece, then floored the vehicle, crossing lanes and the median, then heading in the other direction.

"Bales is at the Museum. My team just spotted him on the camera."

Big Mike held up his phone to a video from the museum security cameras that were obviously working better than they thought. A facial recognition pinpointed Bales in a group of Japanese tourists. He towered over them. Not a very good cover.

"Ramses," Chen said. "That means he didn't get a chariot wheel."

"Is there any security detail at the museum?" Chen wondered.

"We have a team moving in now, but we'll get there first," Big Mike calmly said while zooming down a grassy area around a traffic jam.

Big Mike took an exit that Josh wasn't sure was a legitimate exit or just a way off the main road. Like Tom Cruise in a *Mission Impossible* movie, Big Mike raced around heavy traffic.

Josh first saw the mother holding her baby crossing the street and wondered if they would soon be joining them in the front seat of their SUV. Josh focused on her face and the horror she sensed of her impending death. Big Mike, somehow, swerved like a race car driver and missed a horrible catastrophe.

Big Mike had another job to fall back on if this whole protecting the world thing didn't work out—Hollywood stunt man. He did the best he could in the most difficult of driving conditions Josh had ever seen. Cairo's streets were more parking lots than roads. Somehow Big Mike maneuvered their way to freedom.

Big Mike slipped the vehicle under a closing gate to enter the main parking area. Josh looked back and saw the disgruntled parking attendant shake his fist.

The museum was crowded with buses of tourists from all countries. Big Mike screeched to a halt between two buses. Everyone jumped out in a hurry except Hajj who stayed behind. Josh looked back at him.

"I'll make sure the car is okay," Hajj said.

Josh wondered if that was his main reason.

The team maneuvered through the crowd like a running back racing to the goal line, avoiding collisions with hapless tourists taking pictures of the glorious museum. They pushed right through the ticket area. Josh looked back at the stunned look of the woman from yesterday.

"We were here late yesterday and we're here to get a full day!" Josh cried out as he passed her. She seemed to remember, maybe even okayed it.

Chen pointed to the Ramses area. "Over there." The team continued to slip through the crowd.

Saleem, near the front, slowed down and whispered. "It's right over there. No more attention we need." Everyone downshifted, their eyes on every face in the crowd. Maybe it was a good thing Hajj hadn't come. He would be examining belly buttons at his height.

Josh studied every face, one at a time. His facial recognition moved much more slowly than the museum's.

"Josh," Maria hushed, her eyes guiding Josh to his right. There standing by the body of Ramses was a tall, lean man with a Yankees baseball hat. Josh could see him holding an instrument in his hand, either something that would cut or smash the glass around Ramses.

Josh couldn't help himself. "Bales!" he cried.

Bales returned a look of frustration. Desperately and with little time, he raised the tool over his head but a flash from an Australian tourist's camera standing next to him blinded him.

"Sorry mate. Forgot to turn that off," the tourist apologized, giving Josh time to leap at Bales. Bales pushed Josh away, sending him flying into the tourist. The scuffle caused gasps from the audience.

Bales ran. Josh picked himself up and followed him.

Josh could hear the Australian say "Crikey. Man's having a bad day?"

Bales runs surprisingly fast for an old man, Josh thought. He was thirty yards ahead of them already.

Josh looked behind him. He was followed by Big Mike, Saleem, and then Maria through the back of the museum. No sign of Chen.

Bales pushed through an emergency exit but it didn't sound any alarm.

Josh and the others followed. Now it was a foot race. Bales tapped his ear which could have been an earpiece. He was making a call while running.

Bales was running for the pyramids.

Josh was losing momentum as Big Mike and Maria caught up to him. Josh remembered first seeing Maria jogging so she had some training in the long distance. Saleem slowed to a trot, then leaned over, resting on his knees. He was done.

Josh slowly forgot about his exhaustion seeing the pyramids expand before him. He remembered seeing them before and thinking they were not so impressive from a distance—a big pile of stones—but the closer he got the more magnificent and awesome they appeared. The tourist in him forgot how out of shape he was.

Egyptian guards sitting in chairs and looking at their phones, barely glanced up as a man ran at full speed past them. The sand was particularly difficult to run in.

Why did Bales seem so quick and light? Josh hated him but was impressed by his agility.

Bales ran right at the big pyramid. Crowds gathered around an entrance, it looked like, into the heart of the pyramid. Josh wondered what Bales was thinking.

Bales ran right at the bottom row of rocks. He jumped up and pulled himself to the second row of rocks. Then the third and fourth and …

Bales started climbing the pyramid!

The stones were only around three to four feet high, some five, but their uneven spacing made climbing the huge pyramid … possible … not easy. Bales was going for it.

While Josh couldn't picture Bales' end game—where would he go once he reached the top?—Josh knew Bales was always up to something, with some escape plan formulated, so he followed. He never expected his first encounter with the pyramid to be a climbing expedition.

The climb was surprisingly easy but long. Josh looked back once. Saleem was still bent over his knees and catching his breath. Chen was nowhere to be seen. Maria tried a couple of rocks, then stopped. Big Mike talked on his phone, apparently concocting a better plan.

Bales was not an agile deer leaping from rock to rock during his ascent, but he was steady and persistent. Josh felt like a bull trying to make the climb. He knew he had to be at least thirty years younger than his adversary, so how did Bales maintain his physical dexterity? What powered and motivated him? Josh needed something to keep his mind off the arduous and repetitive climb.

Below, Josh heard the cries and shouts of both encouragement and disapproval from the gathering crowd. Police, who once seemed disinterested in anything, now took great interest in common people deciding to climb their national treasure. Josh knew a camera or two or two hundred were filming him right now and he was sure to be trending on social media.

In the distance, Josh heard a whirring sound approaching. The flap-flap-flap of a propellor. He looked up and saw a helicopter descending from the clouds. Bales was just a few yards from the top. The blades stirred up a dust storm of rocks, dust, and debris that dumped down on Josh, blinding him. He had to turn away.

At the base of the pyramid, the dust storm began to scatter the audience as chunks of ancient rock descended on them.

Josh tried to climb a few more steps but he took the brunt of the storm. He glanced up once and saw a rope ladder fall from the helicopter and Bales grab the first rung. As Josh heard the helicopter depart, he looked up as Bales hung on, halfway up the ladder, looking back and smiling proudly at his accomplishment. The dust storm calmed, and Josh saw he was only one hundred feet from the top.

First a sub, now a helicopter! What's next … a spaceship?

Josh slumped where he was, catching his breath and mourning another lost opportunity. Slowly he took in the view, one he knew few would ever have. He could see the crowds had spread out, brushing themselves off and pouring water in their eyes.

Dejected and exhausted, Josh climbed down the pyramid of Giza. He wondered what he would say and do as the crowds began to close in on him. He could see Saleem and Maria staring at him, compassionately, sorry Josh came up short again. Chen and Hajj appeared next to them to offer support.

Just as Josh was six stones from the bottom, the sounds of sirens approached. The vehicles were black SUVs with lights on the top. They stopped at the base of the pyramid and men with guns stepped out. Their faces were covered with cloth masks and dark sunglasses. They pushed the crowds back ten yards and opened up their car doors to receive their guest.

Josh hopped down from the last rock, wondering now what was going to happen. The men pushed him into the back of the SUV.

For a moment Josh thought he recognized these guys. Their size and stature, the way they carried themselves.

Then he understood as Maria, Saleem, Chen, and Hajj joined him in the car. The men entered the vehicle, slammed the doors and the vehicle sped off.

From the front seat, the leader removed his face mask.

"Everyone okay?" Big Mike asked.

13

The caravan sped away from the pyramids then the three cars split up going in different directions just in case they were being followed.

Josh was a dusty mess, brushing rocks from his hair. Maria gave him water.

"How was the view?" Chen asked.

"Spectacular" was all Josh could say. "But where were you?"

"I went back to the Rameses exhibit to see if Bales got anything. He didn't. The body looked intact. Then I went by to check on Hajj who was all alone in the car. You know in America there are rules against leaving your children in a vehicle."

Hajj pouted. "I'm not a child."

Chen mussed up Hajj's hair. "You are to me, little brother."

"Our cameras confirmed that," Big Mike replied. "Bales got close but did not touch the body."

"What now?" Saleem asked.

Nobody had an answer, so everyone turned to Big Mike. "Since Bales traditionally tries to get as close to the location of the biblical site as possible, we believe the area of east Goshen would be best for us to focus. It's where many archaeologists have been digging."

"If I remember correctly," Chen added, "Pharaoh gave Joseph's family the land in Goshen. That's the area where the Nile spills out, right?"

"And it was fertile land where a group of shepherds would want their sheep to graze," Maria said.

"Avaris. Go to Avaris." Everyone looked at Hajj, who mumbled his response.

Big Mike immediately pressed information into his phone. Chen and Saleem both used their phones to search for more information.

"What is Avaris, Hajj?" Chen asked. "Why should we go there?"

Hajj shrugged.

"I see there were some graves found there," Saleem said, reading from his phone. "Hold on." Saleem read more. "Graves of ancient Jewish people in Egypt! They know they were Jewish because they were buried in a different position than Egyptian people. See."

Saleem held up his phone to a photo he found online. Josh looked more closely. Egyptians it seems from the photo were buried on their backs with their arms to their sides and the Israelites were tucked on their sides into a smaller casket.

"They found bodies of people in this area, and it looks like they were Jewish?" Josh wondered.

"It appears so," Saleem said while reading more information. "Hajj, do you know anything else, like where the digging is taking place?"

The vehicle started to speed up as Josh sensed the urgency and direction now.

Hajj's head sunk lower. "I'm sorry guys."

"No, you stop it Hajj. Everything's fine," Maria said. "We're getting the information we need. You don't have to feel all the pressure." She put her arm around Hajj. "Fear the LORD your God and serve him. Hold fast to him and take your oaths in his name."

"Two hours to Avaris," Big Mike announced. "We're getting the exact location of those graves. My team is contacting the archaeologists."

Everyone sat silently as Big Mike floored it for an hour and a half along a straight shot northeast. Suddenly, near a sign called Al Gharbiyah, Big Mike turned left heading what looked like north to

Josh. Then, just past another hard to pronounce city, they turned left again. The deeper they entered this area once called Goshen, Josh could tell how much greener and more fertile the land was and why the Israelites would want to live here. It was the closest to Israel Josh had seen since they had entered the Middle East.

Josh could feel the car slow down, and Big Mike cautiously scanned the horizon. Josh began looking for himself. He too saw it.

Police cars. Egyptian.

"We've got trouble," Big Mike announced.

The police cars looked authentic, similar to American police vehicles. Black and white with the word "Police" emblazoned across the front. Looked pretty legit.

Four of them blocked the road leading into Avaris. Josh saw the concern on Big Mike's face—does he fight or negotiate or maybe make those electric charges come from his hands like he did in the airport in Tennessee?

Big Mike, surprisingly, slowed the car down and pulled up along-side an Egyptian police officer waving him over.

"Hajj or Chen," Josh said, "Who wants to ..." But before Josh got the words out Big Mike spoke Arabic to the officer.

"Salām 'alaykum," Big Mike said easily.

As the officer responded, Hajj and Chen exchanged looks with everyone in the car. Big Mike speaks Arabic! The exchange seemed pleasant and respectful. Everyone kept quiet, not wanting to give away anything. The officer leaned in and looked at the occupants of the car, studying their faces. Josh was dying to know what they were saying so he looked at Chen and Hajj. Their mouths were agape, unable to believe what they were hearing.

Josh looked to his right, out the window, at the grassy plain. A large grassy field, green and fertile. And standing in that field was a shepherd with his flock. He watched the events transpiring between the two sides with curiosity. And then he saw him.

He's here.

Every time Josh prepared to leave to go to another time, a shepherd, or this shepherd stood out in the open watching him. And there he was, standing in the middle of the grassy plain surrounded by sheep. Josh turned and locked eyes with Maria, who also saw the shepherd.

Slowly Big Mike's conversation got firmer and more direct with fingers pointing and culminating with the Egyptian officer telling them to get out of the car. Big Mike's head dropped slightly and he took a breath. Taking his phone in his hand, he turned to the others.

"Hold on to something, everyone," Big Mike whispered.

Big Mike's big thumb hit a button on the phone. There was a pause and the police officer seemed to reinstate the command to exit the vehicle. Suddenly, the vehicle behind the officer exploded into a fiery ball. Josh thought he saw a rocket come into view, then turned to verify it was a rocket as another blew up the other police car behind it. The officers quickly forgot about Big Mike and started running in the other direction. Luckily none of them were in the vehicles.

Josh turned to see if the shepherd was okay, but there was no sign of him.

Big Mike floored it as another rocket took out the other police car and then another, causing mass distractions. Officers ran in all directions, panicked.

As they drove, everyone sat wide-eyed, trying to figure out what had happened.

"A bit of help from above," was all Big Mike said.

Big Mike raced as the road became dirt, slowing a bit to gain traction. For now, they were clearly out of trouble.

"What happened back there?" Saleem asked.

"The officer said they were looking for someone who fit our description, but didn't say why," Chen said. "Big Mike told them we were on a classified assignment and didn't need to tell them anything. After that things went bad."

"How is his Arabic?" Josh asked.

"Perfect," Hajj replied, surprised.

Everyone looked at Big Mike. "I've had many uses of Arabic in the past."

"Why did you blow them all up," Maria cried, hanging on for dear life.

"They were officers but not working for Egypt. They were hired to keep us out." Big Mike swung a hard left to avoid another officer up the road. "We took out their cars so they won't be following us."

Josh looked up in the sky to see where the attacks had come from. A loud buzz could be heard.

"Drones," was all Big Mike said.

Up ahead they could see the cleared out archaeological dig of Avaris and standing alone in the ruins was a solitary figure.

Bales.

He looked up calmly, seeing the SUV racing toward him. Josh wondered how Bales could be so calm all the time.

Because he's going to win.

The voice sounded more right than ever.

"Is that him?" Saleem asked. "Dr. Bales?"

"Yep," Chen answered.

"He's so ... evil. I can feel it." Saleem looked chilled.

"Big Mike, can you drop a rocket on him?" Hajj asked.

Big Mike shook his head. "We're all out. Wish I could."

As the SUV got closer, Bales calmly placed what he needed in his time travel backpack.

Big Mike floored the vehicle. Fifty feet, forty feet, now thirty feet. Big Mike turned the wheel and slid the SUV as close as he could to the archaeological site.

In one movement and using the momentum of the vehicle, Josh found his car door closest to Bales so he opened it. Physics pushed him forward, rolling him out the door. The move looked cool but Josh regretted doing it because it cost him valuable seconds of reorientation.

As Josh slowly picked himself up off the ground, he heard the familiar whirr of the time machine cranking up.

"Josh, no!" Maria cried from the vehicle. Josh stumbled to his feet and moved in the direction he thought Bales stood, but a dust storm caused by the SUV covered the area. Josh began to regain coherence and found Bales in his haziness. Bales stood thirty feet in front of him as a cloud of dust and heat swirled around him.

"You're always just seconds too late. Always too late," were the last words Bales said.

Josh pushed himself forward, hoping to tackle Bales before he departed.

But he was too late. Josh descended into what felt like his grave as a wave of heat washed over him.

This is hell.

Then everything went dark.

14

Josh sat in the darkness. The walls around him felt close, tight, dirty. His ears rang and his skin felt hot. This place reeked of loneliness and burnt flesh.

Am I in hell?

You should be.

All around him smelled of death. He could move slightly but everything started to spin around him. He was descending deeper and deeper into the pit.

See you soon.

"Josh!" The voice sounded like Maria's but why would she be here in the darkness? She was a good person. A Jesus person.

A hand grabbed him by his shoulder, from the side, from above. Slowly Josh felt the hurt go away—the burning soothe and the oxygen return to his lungs.

He realized the darkness was due to his closed eyes, burned shut, now healing. He felt life and light come back to him, emerging from inside himself. A brightness, cool and soothing, washed over him.

Josh opened his eyes.

A skull stared back at him. Its hollow eye sockets seemed to sense death deep inside Josh, and its response was a wide-jaw laugh.

Josh screamed.

He jumped to his feet, looking around and seeing the three-foot deep stone grave he was laying in.

Saleem's hand reached from above. His healing touch brought life back to Josh's body, now his hand provided assistance to help remove him from the grave. Josh took Saleem's hand and pulled himself up, thankful to get out of this creepy place.

Hajj, Chen, Maria, Saleem, and Big Mike looked Josh over to make sure he was intact and not injured. Their faces still registered the shock they could not shake.

"What happened?" was all Josh could say.

"You don't know what happened?" Chen cried. "You leapt at Bales as he time traveled, throwing yourself into the fireball. You fell into this grave, which probably protected you from total incineration. It was epic."

"We thought you were dead," Maria added, clearly shook up more than the others.

Josh looked down and saw the grave. A skeleton of about five feet long or so laid curled up in the stone sarcophagus.

"Bales must have broken off a part of the skeleton and used it to time travel," Hajj said.

"Look," Saleem pointed at the dead man's hand. "His finger." One of the bodies' fingers was missing.

Big Mike was looking at his phone, as usual. "He didn't find a chariot wheel and he didn't take anything from Ramses the II's body. He chose instead to desecrate an archaeological site and the body of a Jew who was found here in Goshen during the dig."

"So what Babu saw him carrying in the camera footage was the time machine," Maria surmised. All agreed.

"We're looking back at our satellite imagery and Bales traveled light, with no entourage or group of soldiers. It seems he hired a truck to bring him here from the Sea of Aqaba." Big Mike looked disappointed at himself. "Our resources are limited here."

Everyone looked down at the poor soul in the grave whose death could lead to the death of billions if Bales had his way. He had no idea the consequences of his passing and how his body would become part of Bales' super villainous plan.

"Was I dead?' Josh asked.

"Did you feel dead?" Maria asked.

"I didn't feel good. I know that," Josh sighed loudly.

"No, you weren't dead, but badly burned," Saleem said. "We got to you just in time."

Josh looked around at the burn mark surrounding him. The radius went out twenty feet in all directions. "What are we going to do?"

Chen stepped toward Big Mike. "We have to go after him."

Big Mike slowly nodded his head, thinking through everything, as he moved toward the SUV.

"We're going through time?" Saleem exclaimed, his eyes like saucers.

Hajj dipped his head and sulked away. Big Mike walked up to them with the Septagon.

"It's time," Big Mike said. "I had hoped it wouldn't come to this, but you guys have to go."

Josh felt a mixture of excitement and dread. Saleem looked giddy, and Josh knew that feeling but right now he couldn't surrender fully to the rush.

Chen pumped his fist. "Whoa! Moses. The plagues. The sea. This is going to be incredible. It's one of the most talked about time periods in the Bible." Chen took the Septagon from Big Mike. "Let's go!"

"What's wrong with Hajj?" Maria said. "He's acting like he doesn't want to go."

Hajj stood a hundred feet away, sitting on a rock in an overgrown area in the excavation. Josh went over to him.

"What's wrong, Hajj?"

"You guys go ahead. There's no need for me to go. I'm losing my ability that God gave me." Hajj drew in the dirt with his foot.

"Look, when we get there, we need all the help we can get, you know that."

"But what help am I if God can't work through me?"

Josh noticed a tear in Hajj's eye. Hajj quickly wiped it away. Josh always forgot Hajj's age. At his fullest ability, Hajj sounded like an old history professor. Now, Josh could see the real Hajj, eight years old and vulnerable.

"You know I'm new to this whole God-thing, but didn't Chen and the others say something about us having this ability that came from God but it's up to us to manage our hearts and our souls? You're just going through a tough season."

Hajj looked up then immediately back down. Josh glanced over at the others. Maria, Chen, and Saleem appeared to be praying.

Josh continued. "Maybe this adventure will be the confidence you need to move on. This time travel stuff is fascinating, but it's tiring. I know. This will be my third time. I want to make sure this is the last trip we need to take so we need everyone to stop Bales. Including you."

Hajj lifted his head and made eye contact with Josh. Josh felt like he was getting through to him. After a little sniffle, Hajj nodded, appearing slightly more confident or at least ready to go. Josh put his arm around Hajj, his little brother in all this, and walked back to the group. The others surrounded him with love and encouragement.

Saleem put his hand on Hajj's head and peered right into Hajj's eyes. "You must know He is the Rock, his works are perfect, and all his ways are just. A faithful God who does no wrong, upright and just is he. We have to trust him."

Hajj smiled a little, the first Josh had seen in a long time.

"Ready?" Big Mike asked, punching coordinates into his phone.

"What do we do?" Saleem responded. "This is my first time."

Chen held out the Septagon. "Hold on tightly. Once we all get into position, Big Mike fires it up. It will send us through time and deposit us approximately right where we are standing."

"It's very disorienting," Maria said grabbing her spot on the Septagon.

Chen continued. "Definitely, in just a flash everything around you will be like 1400 BC. Everything will be different. The surroundings. The air."

"How does this Septagon work?" Saleem asked. Josh noticed his breathing was accelerating.

"Nobody knows," Chen responded. "Big Mike's organization developed it using some advanced technology. All I know is we can only use it seven times and this is the third."

"As they all say to me all the time—have faith," Josh added.

"Also, there's a time limit on the other side," Hajj barely whispered taking his place on the Septagon.

Chen smiled. "That's right little buddy. Very important to know that. The Septagon remains active for a limited amount of time, revealed in the middle of the Septagon with an LED holographic display. It will tell us the hours, minutes, and seconds we have to use it and return."

"If we don't, we'll be stuck on the other side," Maria cautioned. "There's no way to get back."

"Unless we come get you," Josh said.

"True," Maria agreed. "But that would use up one of our seven time travel allotments. We need to preserve all of them until Dr. Bales is stopped."

"You'll be very thirsty on the other side," Hajj meekly added. "The process dehydrates you."

"Yes. We'll need your healing touch, Saleem," Maria smiled.

Saleem nodded. "I'll do my best."

"We have you all set to arrive in this area of Goshen during the time of Moses. These are our best calculations so hopefully you get there at the right time and place, closer than we've been able to do before." Big Mike seemed to take a deep breath. Josh wondered what

Big Mike thought about all this. He usually seemed so calm. "Once everyone grabs it, the process starts. It's heat activated. "

Chen reached into his pocket and grabbed his cell phone. "Oh, make sure you give your cell phones to Big Mike. They obviously won't work there and anything electronic gets fried in the process. That's why we haven't returned with any pictures." Everyone handed their phones to Big Mike.

Chen, Maria, Saleem, and Hajj were in place, awaiting Josh. But, just as Josh was about to grab the ring, bullets hit the ground around them. Everyone ducked. Their instincts said to run.

Big Mike pulled out a gun from who knows where. "Go! Now!"

A tank and four jeeps came over the hill with their sights set on the gang. Josh hesitated, taking in the spectacle.

"Josh, we need your hand!" Maria cried.

Josh took one more look on the horizon for the shepherd. He wasn't there. Maybe he'll see him again … soon.

Everyone held on as Josh grabbed his spot. The ring began to heat up.

Just as they were about to go, bullets hit Big Mike in the chest and shoulder. He looked dazed as he turned to the group, weak …

Then they were gone.

165 hours – 0 minutes – 0 seconds (Time of day unclear)

Chaos and darkness.

Buzzing and bedlam.

Josh couldn't breathe, couldn't see, couldn't swallow.

The dehydration sucked every ounce of energy from him.

Bad enough Josh dealt with the physical effects of time travel, but to be thrown into this—now—only weakened him further. Everything was so intense, so quick, Josh thought death would be better than this madness.

"Josh!" It sounded like Maria but who could tell in the hurricane of activity swirling around him.

Josh could feel things colliding into him, whipping every inch of his body.

He felt something crawling on his hand, and he brought it up to his face.

A grasshopper?

"It's the plague of locusts!" Saleem screamed. His hand grabbed Josh's arm and suddenly the physical side effects of the time travel went away. The dehydration and recovery that Josh remembered from the last two trips, that seemed to take a day or two to reach normalcy, was suddenly gone in seconds.

Saleem was definitely a valuable part of this group.

"Over here!" It sounded like Chen. Saleem led Josh to the east ... west? It was hard to say. It was hard to know what time of day it was since the locusts blocked the sun.

So many locusts.

"Saleem!" That sounded like Maria. Of course, she wanted him and probably already figured out he could make her feel better. Josh and Saleem shielded their faces and found Maria, hiding behind a rock, covered in creepy, crawly locusts. Saleem touched her and her eyes rolled, taking a huge gasp of relief. She shook it off then cried out, "Hajj is over here!"

Maria led them to Hajj lying on the ground with his hands over his head. Josh got to him first.

"Hajj, we're here. It's going to be okay!"

Saleem jumped in and one touch, boom. Hajj lifted his head like waking up refreshed from a nap. His first words, "Where's Chen?"

Everyone started crying Chen's name until Maria motioned for them to come over by something that looked like a tree, now stripped of leaves.

Chen rolled in agony on the ground. They turned him over. His face looked horrified and his mouth open as a locust crawled out. Everyone gasped and jumped back. Saleem, though, jumped in and applied his magic touch. Chen spit the locust out then jumped to his feet, hopping and brushing himself off. "I hate bugs! Did I ever tell you that?"

The others actually laughed. Thanks to Saleem they felt good enough to laugh, and Chen just looked so funny covered with bugs.

"Over here!" Maria yelled, pointing to something ahead of her. As they moved closer they found a tent, about twelve feet by twelve feet. They jumped inside.

It was abandoned, thankfully.

> So Moses stretched out his staff over Egypt, and the LORD made an east wind blow across the land all that day and all that night. By morning the wind had brought the locusts; they invaded all Egypt and settled down in every area of the country in great numbers. Never before had there been such a plague of locusts, nor will there ever be again. They covered all the ground until it was black. They devoured all that was left after the hail—everything growing in the fields and the fruit on the trees. Nothing green remained on tree or plant in all the land of Egypt.
>
> Exodus 10:13–15

Inside, everyone took a moment to reorient and take a breath. They could hear the buzzing outside and the sounds of locusts hitting the tent, but the animal skin covering shielded them and muffled the sound.

"How long does this go on?" Saleem asked.

"Hard to say," Chen replied. "I think a day, right Hajj?"

"Yeah, the scripture says one whole day and night...I think." *Wow, Hajj never used those words "I think,"* Josh thought. *He used to be so sure.*

In all of the chaos, Josh lost track of the Septagon. He asked around. Nobody had it. It must still be outside with all those icky locusts.

"I'll go," Saleem offered. He found a blanket on the ground, part of a bed that was abandoned quickly, and ran outside. Four minutes later, Saleem ran in, covered with locusts. Chen and Josh brushed the locusts off, then stepped on the locusts, crunching them under their feet. In less than one minute, the three of them killed twenty-six insects.

Saleem revealed the Septagon in his hand. It read *164 hours – 45 minutes – 22 seconds*. They had only been here fifteen minutes and already Josh felt exhausted. He laid down on the blankets used as a bed and fell asleep.

153 hours – 52 minutes – 7 seconds
(Time of day unclear)

Josh woke startled. He took a breath, reorienting himself.

Everyone else started to wake up too. Josh felt great, remembering how hard it was the last two times to recover from the time travel.

"Saleem, thanks for healing us," Josh said. "You don't know how hard it is to recover from the time travel."

"I can tell," he replied. "When God heals someone through me, I can feel the degree of pain and healing briefly as the power goes through my body. It was pretty intense for each of you."

"Do you heal yourself?" Chen asked.

"So far, yes. I simply grab my wrist and pray, then I'm all better," Saleem smiled. He seemed genuinely honored to have this power, while Josh felt cursed at times with his visions.

Maria held up the Septagon. "150 hours means just a few hours short of one week. That's a long time here," Maria said, looking around the tent for the solution to her next question. "We need to find some disguises or clothes to wear so we can walk around."

The family that left this tent could have been Egyptians, poor ones, the five of them were unsure. However, they had enough clothing to go around. Josh was ecstatic he didn't have to dress up like he did in Iran. Instead Maria pointed out that these long pieces of fabric were linen and meant to wrap around the body. Josh hoped they wore it correctly. But after a huge locust infestation, Josh guessed nobody cared about fashion.

Then Josh remembered … "Big Mike!"

"I saw it too," Chen replied. "He was shot as we slipped back in time."

Hajj looked like he was going cry. "I thought that's what I saw too. No way."

Maria and Saleem hadn't seen it happen as the others recounted what they saw. The group sat quietly for a moment.

"Big Man can handle himself," Chen said. "Remember, he stepped out of a helicopter crash." Josh remembered that. The guy was indestructible. That memory certainly helped everyone cope as they told Saleem what happened last time.

"Yeah, a bullet to the chest is a like a mosquito bite to that guy," Josh smiled.

"That poor bullet didn't have a chance up against Big Mike," Hajj said. Everyone laughed.

Chen led a prayer for Big Mike, all of them hoping for the best.

Outside the locusts continued to buzz and crash into the animal hide tent which worked surprisingly well as a barrier. A few locusts crawled in to check things out and someone either stomped the critter or pushed it away.

"This is the eighth plague," Hajj announced as they sat around waiting. "Darkness is next. We need to make sure we are out of the Egyptian territory when that happens."

"I remember the Bible text that said it was only dark in the Egyptian areas, but not the Israelite areas," Chen reminded them.

Maria turned to Josh. "You've experienced that darkness in a vision. It's bad."

Josh took a breath, remembering. Locusts were a mess but the darkness was horrible—lonely and confusing. He hated that feeling from those visions.

"We need to wait out these locusts then we can head out before the next plague and find Moses," Maria said, making herself comfortable on the ground with a blanket. "Bales probably is keeping his distance until this plague is over too."

Nobody knew the time and the blanket of locusts in the sky hid whether it was day or night. Josh peeked out and saw either a dim sun or a bright moon shining in the sky. It made everyone tired.

Everyone found their place in the tent and went back to sleep. Nobody seemed worried about the owner of the house returning.

Josh fell asleep with the Septagon on his chest.

145 hours – 18 minutes – 52 seconds (Morning)

Josh woke up and stared at the clock in his face. He had slept hard and woke up disoriented. Chen was gone as well as Hajj. Maria and Saleem slept soundly. He tucked the Septagon into his backpack for safekeeping. It would be a while until they needed it again.

Josh stepped out of the tent and saw Chen and Hajj talking. It was morning. Peaceful and serene, like the calm after a storm.

If it wasn't for the millions of dead locusts on the ground you wouldn't have thought anything happened last night. Josh noticed how quiet nature was, devastated and in shock by yesterday's plague. Then he could see off in the distance what was preoccupying the birds—it was an all-you-can-eat feast. Dead locusts make for a wonderful breakfast and thousands of birds were dining on the carcasses all around them. This place should be picked clean by evening. Then tomorrow, lots of fat birds will try to lift themselves off the ground.

Josh walked toward Hajj and Chen, every step a crunchy delight. They stopped talking when Josh approached.

"Crazy, huh?" Josh said, indicating the insect graveyard all around them.

"Yeah. Easily millions of locusts converged on this area yesterday," Chen replied.

Josh turned to Hajj. "Anything we need to know about locusts?"

"Well, they are from the grasshopper family, Acrididae. Locusts live solitary lives, but when the right conditions happen, like drought, they band together into these swarms and work together to eat everything they can find. The Egyptian crops have to all be picked clean," Hajj added. He took a breath, looking happy he got that all out.

"Thanks for that," Josh said. "What were you guys talking about when I walked up? Sorry I interrupted."

"Oh, we were having a little devotional time, talking about God. We need that to keep our spiritual gifts active, right Hajj?" Chen said, tapping Hajj on the back … his little brother.

Hajj agreed and smiled looking more confident. By this time, Maria and Saleem emerged from the tent and entered the conversation.

Hajj rubbed his face, preparing to make a confession. "I think what happened is that I got so angry at Ishmael that I let my emotions drive my faith. I wanted to change history because I thought God needed me too. Then, when we arrived back in our time, God was working on my parents' hearts. God didn't need me, but what I forgot is that I need Him." Hajj dipped his face into his hands. Maria crossed over and hugged Hajj, applauding him for his revelation.

Josh had no basis of understanding any of this. He had this gift but no faith.

Or maybe he had faith but didn't quite understand it.

No, you don't have faith. You're hopelessly lost.

"What should we do now?" Saleem asked.

"Eat," Josh answered.

Chen picked up a dead locust. "It's full of protein." Chen popped it in his mouth and chewed away. He pulled a locust leg out of his teeth and flicked it to the ground.

Everyone gagged and protested but as they did, they came to the realization that Chen was right. There was no food in the tent and no other tent around as far as the eye could see.

Chen took another crunchy bite, then another. He put a total of five in his mouth. "Not bad. No real taste. Could use some chocolate."

Saleem went second. "I've actually had them before." He, too, popped two or three into his mouth.

Maria and Hajj followed taking cautious bites then realizing locusts weren't so bad if you didn't look at what you were eating.

Josh looked down at the one in hand. Its wing quivered a bit. It's alive. Josh thought it looked like a cockroach on steroids. He put it down. "Nope."

Now everyone was chowing down on at least four or five locusts each.

Josh gagged, but he was so hungry. He closed his eyes and slowly brought the hopefully dead locust to his mouth. In it went.

He chewed it quickly, feeling the insides burst with a splashy squirt inside his mouth. Then he came to the realization—it wasn't terrible. Josh didn't chow down like he was a buffet line, but he ate three more over the next fifteen minutes.

As they ate, Maria asked a question. "I thought the Septagon deposited us more accurately in the time and space we needed. Since we were at an Israelite archaeological site, shouldn't we have shown up in the Israelite side of town where there wouldn't have been locusts?"

Hajj took a bite then replied with his mouth full. "I wondered about that too. But I'm glad we didn't show up in the middle of the Israelite camp which has like a million people inside it. That tells me for our safety they had us materialize outside the camp where nobody could see us and unfortunately that means right in the middle of the plagues."

"Hopefully we are close to the Israelites?" Saleem asked.

"I hope so," Chen said. "When we're done eating, let's see what we can find." He popped another locust in his mouth. That was like his tenth one. Yuck!

139 hours – 6 minutes – 6 seconds
(Afternoon)

The group headed north, northwest looking for signs of life.

All they found was devastation and abandonment. The plagues had successfully punished Egypt for their hard-heartedness. They found dead animals and dead people along the way. And of course, dead locusts. Josh previously ate the dead locusts but he considered them "fresh." Consuming a dead locust sitting in the hot sun didn't seem very appetizing.

But there was nothing to be found to eat wherever they went. The locusts consumed every crop, every tree, the contents of every basket. Hunger was starting to creep in for the team. Twenty or so locusts didn't exactly fill you. It was like eating twenty potato chips. They needed to find civilization fast.

Chen reminded them along the way what had happened in the time-line of Moses after the eighth plague of locusts. According to the Bible, Pharaoh talked to Moses and confessed his sinfulness and asked for forgiveness. Moses prayed and God waved the locust infestation away. But, once again, Pharaoh refused to let the people go.

"Wow," Josh said. "This Pharaoh is stubborn. Has he seen this devastation?"

"He's no different than Bales," Maria added. "Bales has failed twice in trying to stop biblical history and yet, here we are again … trying to stop him from getting to Moses."

"Plus God hardened Pharaoh's heart," Hajj said meekly.

Josh stopped, shocked by what he heard. "Wait, what?" Are you saying God made Pharaoh stubborn? So does that mean it's God's fault this is happening?"

Nobody answered right away.

"No, we're definitely not saying that," Maria replied. "Pharaoh was already stubborn, but God made him super-stubborn to make the story even greater."

"To make the story greater? God makes people super-stubborn so God can look like Superman? Hmm, I don't like that." Josh could feel his resistance to God grow stronger every time he heard things like this.

"People need great displays of God's power to believe," Chen said. "That's why there were ten plagues, not two or three. This is one of the most talked about stories in the Bible. It showed what God could do, His power over nature."

Josh shook his head. "There has to be other ways."

"If there was, I'm sure God thought about them," Hajj said. Everyone turned to Hajj who nobody expected to say something so profound. Chen caught up to Hajj and put his arm around him.

"Well said," Chen said, encouraging his little brother.

"What's that?" Saleem pointed off to the left. Everyone ducked but there was nothing to hide behind.

A small family of six walked with their belongings.

"Where are they headed?" Josh asked.

"Good question. Probably to find help or food." Maria paused and seemed to pray silently for a moment. Then stood up. "Let's follow them."

It was the break they needed.

But Josh couldn't shake this idea that God made people stubborn, more evil—people like Bales who would kill Josh's family (or whatever happened to them)—just so he could get more kudos.

It's why he couldn't believe.

134 hours – 55 minutes – 23 seconds (Afternoon)

"There it is!" Chen was the first to see it.

This was obviously an Egyptian city. As the group walked closer to it, Josh could see the city extended for a mile in each direction. The buildings were constructed of stone, making it feel massive and solid. While the buildings looked no more than two or three stories high, certain structures jutted out from the horizon, mostly statues of gods or important people.

Mansions lined the banks of the Nile, and in the center of the city stood a massive temple.

"Hajj, what are we looking at?" Chen shouted.

Hajj seemed to struggle with words, but after a moment of hesitation he began to talk. "This is Pi-Ramesses, which means the House of Ramses. It's the new capital he built by Avaris where we were earlier. Ramses grew up in this area, which is probably why he moved his capital north. It was likely to have a population of 300,000 people." Hajj finished his analysis, took a breath and looked relieved. The old Hajj was coming back.

Also recognizable as they entered the city was the destruction they had just faced. This once pristine city looked worn and battered.

Various people walked about, looking beaten and defeated. The garbs worn by Josh and the others fit in perfectly, because everyone's clothes were torn in some way or had blood on them. The groups who walked together weren't talking to each other, probably not knowing what to say. There was very little interaction between people passing by each other, maybe a glance to see if the other was okay or if they looked worse than the other felt.

Saleem and Maria pointed out various signs of the past plagues. Red stains on the riverbanks and on the walls of the riverfront homes. Skeletons of dead frogs and bodies of rotting livestock in the streets. The hail punched dings in almost every building. Nothing didn't have a pock mark on it. Then, of course, the dead locusts. Birds marched aerially above the city, diving down to grab a bite. Nobody shooed the birds away because they were doing a public service and cleaning the place up.

It reminded Josh of the garbage dumps he had seen where birds flew to dine. The smell Josh sensed matched the smell of those dumps: rotting death.

As they entered the city, they saw some Egyptians in the streets crying or sitting against walls dazed and lost. Little bits of conversations happened.

Josh asked, "Chen, what are they saying?"

Chen listened then replied, "I can understand them pretty clearly, can you Hajj?"

Hajj nodded. "Yes, it's close to my language. I can understand parts."

Chen listened again. "They are talking about the destruction. Some seem very upset at Pharaoh wondering why he won't let the Israelites go. And others ..." Chen listened carefully. "Others are saying this Moses is a god. Lots of talk about Moses. They respect him."

"If we find Pharaoh, we are most likely to find Moses, right? Moses marches into the city from outside. And where Moses is, Bales will likely be nearby." Josh's assessment seemed good to the others.

"Let me see what I can do," Chen hid his face under his clothing. Others were masking themselves because of the smell and it worked perfectly for Chen to hide himself. He crossed over to a man overseeing, what looked like, a garage sale of stuff. Chen asked him a question. The man, in shock, pointed to the north. Chen thanked him and returned to the group. "He said Pharaoh's palace is that way, near the huge temple we saw. We're almost there."

"How did he seem?" Saleem asked.

"Traumatized," Chen replied.

"The worst is yet to come," Maria said as they moved through the streets.

In addition to the psychological state of the Egyptians, it was easy to notice the spiritual state of this vast city—they loved their gods. All kinds of temples, obelisks, statues, and sphinxes were on every street and block.

Some of this looked familiar.

"It's him!" Maria pointed out. "I remember this. We were rushing into the museum and this was standing there with three or four others that were huge."

The thirty-foot tall statute of Ramses they rushed by in the Grand Egyptian Museum was staring right at them. Everyone stopped to gawk at it. Josh clearly remembered it. "Man, I wish I had a camera."

His attention shifted to a group of people who seemed to be watching them. Josh couldn't understand why. They matched the dress code. People either looked like peasants, like they did, or Egyptian royalty.

Egyptian style was more clean shaven with white linen and gold accessories. The upper-class men and women had jet black hair cut with high bangs and long sides. They looked like runway fashion models except for their sad, confused faces.

Other peasants, like themselves, wore the same cooler linens but few covered their heads as they were doing. Maybe that made them stand out. They needed to adjust but didn't want their faces to give them away. Maria could possibly pass for Middle Eastern with her Hispanic looks. Hajj definitely. Saleem ... maybe. But Chen and Josh stood out and jeopardized the group. Better just to keep moving and hiding in the shadows.

A group of four people fought over a basket of food creating a lot of attention. Josh steered them down an alley. As they walked between the two buildings they realized it was a dead end.

"My bad," Josh said but as they turned around, they found the way blocked by the group of four men who were studying them.

The leader, who appeared to be a soldier, spoke up. The four men created a wall and they would not win by charging through them. It seemed that he just asked a question. Chen stepped forward and spoke.

The men listened then asked another question. Chen spoke this time with more volume and pointing his finger at the men's chests. Fear washed over them and these four Egyptians stripped off their gold and threw it all at the feet of Chen. Then, they ran away.

"What did you say," Saleem said, chuckling.

"They asked who we were and what we were doing. I said we were Israelite spies and God was about to rain down another plague on them if they dared laid a hand on us! They gave us ... presents." Chen picked up a bracelet, examining it. "We can buy some food with this." Chen put it on.

Everyone else found something and put it on also, so they could fit in better with the locals wearing some bling.

"They are a lot nicer than the men at Sodom and Gomorrah," Josh said, leaning over to Hajj.

"A lot nicer," Hajj re-emphasized.

The five of them felt more confident and entered the main street. Not many shops were open and there was no food to be found.

"By this time, eight plagues in," Hajj said. "The people are starving."

Chen asked a few more Egyptians for directions and eventually they found the palace. Guards stood outside but they didn't look very tough. Even they had had enough with all the current events, talking to each other, leaning against the stone pillars, letting people pass with barely a glance. Nothing seemed to matter much to them any longer. The group used their laziness to their advantage and snuck in.

The stairs into the palace led right to the main room where Pharaoh himself held court, sitting on an ornate gold throne. Josh expected a sort of formality, kind of like when a president sits in the room but the recent events changed the atmosphere of royalty. People sat in groups talking, crying, mourning. Onlookers, like Josh and his friends, just wandered in, probably never having a chance to see Pharaoh in action.

Josh saw another group of men, far off in a corner, wearing ornate and fantastic costuming which Chen immediately identified and whispered to the others. "The magicians." They looked beaten, still recovering, Chen said, from their boils. They itched themselves, like Josh remembered when he had chicken pox. Their bodies were covered with red pimples.

And then there was Pharaoh. Pharaoh looked ... tired. Like most Egyptians his skin had a darker complexion, like Hajj and most Middle Easterners. Josh doubted he got out in the sun for any reason, living in this beauti-

> The magicians could not stand before Moses because of the boils that were on them and on all the Egyptians.
>
> Exodus 9:11

ful golden prison. He wore a long flowing robe, wrapped around him. It looked like he had eyeliner or some kind of make-up on him to accent his cheeks and eyes, but it was worn and dabbled from lack of care or maybe just crying.

Pharaoh sat on his throne, his head resting on one hand, listening to some sort of counsel from a man who seemed very upset and whose finger pointed numerous times at Pharaoh. However, Pharaoh seemed to take it, looking lost. After a minute of ranting, the man stopped seeing it was going nowhere. Pharaoh nodded then waved the man away.

Chen whispered to the group, "The man was telling Pharaoh to let the people go because the city could not take any more devastation. No water. No food. Pharaoh seems very tired."

Maria turned to Hajj, "Can you understand any of their talk?"

"Yes," Hajj told her. "I hear pieces of my language, which helps me to understand the bigger picture, but not enough to interpret like Chen."

Pharaoh sat alone on the throne. Nobody bothered him for ten minutes or so.

Saleem huddled everyone together. "What should we do?"

"Let's not forget why we are here," Chen replied. "We have to find Bales. I think he would fit in more here in this city, Pi-Ramesses, than in the Jewish city, Avaris. This is an easier place to hide amongst all the chaos."

Josh chimed in. "Yes, but didn't someone say there were over a million people in the Jewish camp. That seems easy to hide in."

"Yes, but the Israelites are very protective of their people," Hajj offered. "Plus they sleep in tents, with their families. Bales is a loner. It would stand out."

"Don't underestimate Bales. Remember, he hid on the anchor outside Noah's ark during the storm," Josh recalled. "He's stubborn."

"Why don't we look around a little and see if he's here," Saleem said, so they took a little tour and kept their eyes open.

"Uh-oh," Chen said looking over their shoulders. Everyone turned. Pharaoh was looking right at them. Josh wondered what they would do if he called them forward. Chen put his right hand to his heart and bowed. Josh did the same, so did the others as they backed up. Pharaoh kept his eye on them then eventually lost interest.

The group turned a corner and sighed. "That was close," Josh said.

For the next hour they walked around the palace but saw no sign of Bales. Pharaoh's soldiers, who would have likely stopped them, were so worn out and distracted, the team practically had free access to the palace.

"Let's find the Israelite camp. We need to establish a presence there too. This place seems tired," Maria said.

Everyone agreed. Chen asked for directions and people pointed northeast. They walked in that direction and it wasn't long until they saw the city. A massive gathering of easily a million people were in the streets. And the mood there was quite different than in Egypt.

129 hours – 2 minutes – 55 seconds
(Early evening)

As Josh and the group entered the city, they walked into a party. Well, compared to the Egyptian section they just visited, this was a party. The people were talking, laughing, engaged with one another. Kids played, chased goats, and giggled the whole time.

And there was food. The sight of it made Josh's stomach immediately flip-flop. He hadn't really thought about food since seeing the devastation in Pi-Ramesses but now seeing—and smelling—food sparked a need for it. The Israelites had baskets of cucumbers, melons, onions, and garlic. The group's faces must have shown their want because an older lady offered Josh a plate.

Josh looked to the others, especially Chen, who recognized he was needed. Chen walked up to her and began talking. His hands folded in appreciation. He looked gracious then the old woman made four more plates for the others. Everyone smiled and bowed, thumping their chests, hoping that translated into their culture. They gave her a piece of the gold they had been given in exchange for the food.

They walked off a few steps and sat down, away from the others and ate.

"It really tastes good. So fresh!" Saleem cried.

"Yes, we've noticed that after three trips into the past. Better food quality," Chen replied.

"Chen, what was the woman saying?" Josh asked, taking another bite of cucumber.

"Apparently we look Egyptian, but that's okay. There are other Egyptians here who have switched sides and see the Israelite God as the one and only God. She said we looked hungry and offered us food."

"Is it that obvious?" Maria bit into an onion, eating it like an apple. "This is the best onion I've ever bitten into and I've never bitten into an onion."

Everyone walked by them and were very welcoming. Josh felt at home here, kind of like the atmosphere he felt at Maria's house. A big happy family.

Josh looked around and could see the houses—thousands of them. They had a stone construction, not the chiseled marble they saw in Pi-Ramesses. The roofs were made of thatch and wood frames held the windows and doors.

It felt late, like dinner time.

"The people here go to bed around sundown, so we need to find a place to crash," Hajj said.

"I would love to find Moses," Josh said, stepping up on his tiptoes to try.

Maria shook her head. "If we're seen as outsiders, I don't think we should seem too anxious to see Moses."

"How about asking around about Bales?" Saleem offered.

"Too risky and too many people. We haven't seen him yet and have no idea what he is wearing," Chen replied.

"He is tall," Josh remembered.

From somewhere a thousand feet away, maybe a half mile, a disturbance started to build within the people. Like a wave rolling in, it closed in around them.

Praise.

People stopped what they were doing and raised their hands, singing in unison. The words seemed to repeat but nobody really cared.

Chen, Saleem, and Maria stood and raised their hands like many others. Hajj slowly joined in, and Josh could tell it was helping him. Josh, though, had no frame of reference. He faked his response to fit in.

"What's going on?" Josh asked.

Chen slipped out of his corporate praise mode. "Praise. People just praising God. It's magnificent."

Josh waited patiently. After about five minutes the words faded and drifted away. The Israelites smiled and encouraged one another, hugging and kissing, then entering their homes over the next thirty minutes.

"What are we going to do?" Josh asked.

"I've been praying," Maria said. "God will answer."

It took another five minutes but two men walked toward them with a tent. Chen talked to them. Again he looked appreciative and the two Israelites insisted and were gracious. The men set the tent up, inviting the group to stay inside.

Two women, presumedly their wives, walked up with blankets.

While Chen and Hajj thanked their hosts, Josh saw him.

A mirage? A dream? A vision? No, this was real.

Bales saw Josh first, and Bales actually looked shocked. Josh returned the shocked look. Each of them froze not knowing what to do next.

"It's him," Josh hushed, jumping to his feet and racing into the crowd. He didn't look back to see if anyone was following him.

At the moment of visual connection, Bales was easily fifty yards away, down a long street. He slipped down an ally when Josh sprinted toward him so Josh tried to anticipate his route. After slipping down other streets and checking every place he could, Josh came up empty.

The others ran up, out of breath.

"You saw him?" Hajj huffed.

"Yes," Josh replied, now realizing he too was out of breath.

"Are you sure?" Josh at first felt offended that Maria would ask such a question.

"We looked right at each other. I'm sure."

"Do we keep looking around for him?" Saleem asked. "It's getting dark."

"I don't know how this town would respond to a bunch of outsiders walking around the town at night," Chen wisely stated. "I'm sure Bales won't be lurking around either. He probably just saw an opportunity and looked around. Everyone will be going to bed for the night."

Josh looked around realizing just how huge this town was. The streets were thinning of people entering their homes. It was twilight.

"Let's go," Josh said, turning and walking down the street. Then he realized, "Is this the right way?"

The others weren't sure either, but together they found the tent that had been set up by their hosts.

Four of the group slept soundly in the tight quarters. But not Josh. He couldn't get that face out of his mind.

117 hours – 22 minutes – 8 seconds (Morning)

Josh got up before the others and stood outside the tent scanning the horizon for another possible glimpse of his enemy. He hoped Bales would return to make sure he saw what he saw. Getting into the mind of Bales and trying to figure out what he would do next was difficult this time especially with the absence of visions, which Josh normally hated, but right now wished for one.

His visions have gone dark.

It was twilight, a hint of light from the sun on the eastern horizon announcing its arrival. Josh could still see the stars that were so bright and so clear in this ancient world. He could see so much detail in the sky—planets, stars, the Milky Way. No wonder people back then believed in God. The solar system spoke to him. Maybe, that's why Josh felt he loved to look at the stars.

He felt small on this earth but not alone. He just basked in the vastness of space. It took his breath away. How did this all come to be?

It means nothing.

"See anything?" Saleem's calm voice frightened Josh who was lost in another dimension of thought.

"No. It's quiet out here." Josh could see people starting to stir and step outside to stretch and take a breath of fresh morning air. The horizon was filling with groggy people.

"So Maria says this man, Bales, killed your mom and your father? Is that right?"

"Maybe. Most likely. I believe he had something to do with the death of my mother. And he kidnapped my father and has been claiming he hid him somewhere."

Saleem shook his head in disbelief. "I can't imagine how that feels. I guess I would want him dead too." Then after a moment, he asked. "Why do you think he came to this time?"

"I'm not sure. If we look at the pattern of Noah, Abraham, and now Moses, I think he's just trying to take out the greatest men of the Bible, right? Without any of them, everything falls apart."

"Yes, that's true, but for some reason it seems like it's more than that."

Josh turned to Saleem, waiting for an explanation. When Saleem did not answer, Josh asked, "What do you mean?"

"I'm not sure. But it seems to me that when evil is evil, it's more complicated than what it appears on the surface. Evil is never so simple."

"I just thought he wanted to rule the world."

Saleem smiled. "Don't we all. Sin is all about control and authority. We all want to rule our world. That's how we got into this mess." Those words hung in the air for a moment, when Chen pushed back the tent flap.

"Did they have coffee in the time of Moses?"

From inside, Hajj said, "No."

Chen looked like he could cry.

Later, their hosts came by with warm bread that was probably the best bread anyone had ever tasted. They didn't even miss the traditional slab of butter.

While everyone chatted about their observations of this time period, something like 1400 BC, Josh could not get his mind off of Bales. The argument raged in his head.

Do you think you can stop him?

Maybe. I'm the only one motivated enough to take him out. Everyone else is on a field trip, but I have the most important reason to stop Bales.

Seeing Bales confirmed to Josh that they were where they needed to be. This is why they have travelled through time to find him and stop him.

Go!

Josh hated that voice but sometimes it made sense.

When the group seemed playfully engaged with a group of children, Josh slipped away. No vision called him. Just instinct. And passion.

110 hours – 3 minutes – 31 seconds (Afternoon)

Josh knew it was risky traveling outside the camp, especially not knowing the language, but he figured he could act like a mute or something. That somehow felt like a biblical thing to do.

But he really felt like Bales would feel more comfortable in Egyptian territory, his people. Those who were anti-God.

Josh paid attention to the surroundings as they walked into Avaris a day ago, taking in the landmarks just in case he needed to travel between the cities. Maybe he always knew he would run away from the others … again.

This time Josh didn't feel like he was abandoning his friends, but accomplishing the mission. Find Bales. Stop him. Whatever it takes.

You are doing the right thing.

A dozen or so people passed by other Egyptians migrating to the Jewish camp, but nobody was following the route he followed, entering Pi-Ramesses.

Again, the guards didn't seem intent on keeping anyone in or out of the city, so Josh walked right in. The city looked much like it did the day before. Lots of confused and distraught people shuffling along doing their routines, looking like they weren't sure what to do anymore.

Josh felt like he walked every street imaginable and looked at every face he could.

They must think I'm some kind of weirdo.

To say finding Bales was an obsession was an understatement. Thankfully the streets had some degree of symmetry to them, so he could walk up one in a fairly straight line then walk down another. After three hours, Josh wondered what he was doing here.

This is stupid. I should have stayed with the others. Go back. Now!

As Josh began to plan an exit strategy and head home, a man ran down the street screaming something in a language Josh didn't understand. The people listened to him and asked questions. He answered, and they began to cry. The man ran right up to Josh, grabbing his shoulders and gently shaking him.

His words sounded desperate and sad. The man began to cry and fell into Josh's arms. Josh suddenly found himself comforting the man, hugging him, and patting him on the back. The man released his grip, bowed his head to Josh and said something in the tone of "Thank you," then went on his way.

The city was quite a contradiction to Sodom and Gomorrah. Sodom and Gomorrah felt like a perpetual selfish party. Here they were far more humble, focused on survival more than pleasure.

The others told Josh things were about to get worse. These Egyptians had no idea the fate that they were facing. This town, beaten by eight plagues, felt surrendered to their imminent death.

Josh looked to the sky, checked out the streets then determined the way home. He crossed one block. A man came down the street perpendicular to Josh's and nearly ran into him. Josh wanted to say "excuse me" but it didn't translate well here.

Then he realized who the man was.

Bales.

Standing ten feet from each other, the two took five seconds to assess that this was really happening. Bales smiled his toothy grin. Josh gritted his teeth.

"You have a knack for being in the wrong place at the wrong time," Bales hissed.

"It feels like the right time if you're here," Josh countered.

"We do seem to cross paths regularly. Almost as if someone wants us to see each other. Do you believe in that 'someone' yet?" Bales asked. A couple walked by and Josh and Bales stopped talking until they were a few steps away.

"I believe in what I see and right now I see a murderer and a kidnapper, and I'm here to take you back to the authorities in our time."

Bales looked amused. "Sometimes you need help to see." Bales pulled out a set of goggles. They had a two adjustable, something Josh had seen before, on TV or the movies.

Bales adjusted the goggles, tapped a few buttons on them and said, "Good night, Josh. It's time." Bales began walking away. Josh leapt at him, hoping to grab an arm or something.

But that's when everything went dark.

And it wasn't a vision.

101 hours – 48 minutes – 6 seconds (Darkness)

Josh could see absolutely nothing. It wasn't just night, with a silvery moon in the sky, ricocheting traces of light to the earth, this was darkness, the complete absence of any light.

Josh had heard the expression, "You couldn't see your hand in front of your face" and always thought that was an exaggeration. But he literally could not see his hand in front of his face.

Minutes after Bales left, Josh realized Bales had brought night vision glasses through time. He actually knew the Bible better and believed it more literally, and came prepared. Now Bales had the ability to walk around with an advantage, a ghost in the dark who could see his every move.

In fact, maybe he's watching me now?

Josh looked to his left and right but it made no difference. He couldn't see a thing.

He could hear well, and all he heard were screams and cries. The screams of an entire city in the worst possible blackout imaginable.

Josh crawled on his hands and knees, bashing his head against a wall. The impact dazed Josh. He felt his head and sensed blood ... or was it water? So crawling won't work. Josh stood.

With his arms extended, Josh took tiny steps in the darkness, finding a wall then using it to guide his path. He tripped over a tool or a bucket and fell hard to the ground, again hitting his head against something.

Now Josh realized he had to walk with one hand against the wall, one hand extended and kicking his feet forward in case something was in his path. In the light, Josh imagined how silly he looked.

This worked for a half hour or so until Josh asked himself …

Where are you going?

He really had no idea. Josh was just going, doing something, getting somewhere. He figured this darkness had to end somewhere.

Josh remembered that the Israelite camp suffered no ill effects of the plagues. There had to be light there.

But how can he find it?

His foot felt something in his path. Josh reached down and felt the soft, wet object.

It was a face…bleeding.

Josh recoiled, stumbling backwards over his own feet and smacking the ground hard. There were hurt or perhaps even dead people in his path. Josh's scream joined the symphony of screams in the city all around. Probably they too just discovered a dead person, or fell hitting their heads, or just emotionally felt the loneliness of darkness.

This was hell.

Josh found a corner in a building and sat down. It felt like a secure place.

Despair overtook Josh, and he began to cry. He hadn't sobbed like this since he got the news that his mom had died.

Now the last visual image in his mind, the last thing he saw before the lights went out, was the man he believed had killed his mom and most likely his dad.

The crying lasted ten, fifteen minutes, it was hard to tell in the dark, and Josh drifted off to sleep.

? hours – ? minutes – ? seconds
(Darkness)

Josh jolted awake as something brushed by him, then started licking him. He grabbed the thing by his tiny horns. It fought Josh, wanting to be free. Josh clutched the little guy close to his chest. It was a goat.

Can goats see in the dark?

It would be nice if Hajj were around to ask that question but Josh had to assume they could since the goat found him. A rope extended around the goat's neck. It had obviously been tied up and had broken free in the chaos.

Josh grabbed the rope, wrapping it once around his hand for security, then released the animal. The goat pulled him in some direction, scampering to his next adventure.

Josh had a seeing-eye goat.

He made sure he gave the goat enough flexibility to go where it wanted to go, but kept the goat close enough to follow his tracks. Within minutes, Josh could feel the personality and relationship of his friend.

The cries and screams had decreased to a low moan. Josh passed by the moaners not wanting to engage them, fearing panic and attack, like a drowning man may do to his rescuer.

Josh thought about the previous plagues that ravaged this town. Boils and hail would definitely hurt. Losing livestock and their water supply definitely created hunger and thirst. But darkness ... this created a mental issue.

The worst punishment in a prison, Josh heard, was solitary confinement. Prison yards and cells had at least some interaction in their confinement. Solitary cut off any relationship or hope of any relationship and sometimes blacked out all the lights. Josh didn't know how long they kept people in solitary confinement but he couldn't imagine longer than this. How much time had passed? Five hours? Five days?

Then again, Josh thought, this is how blind people live. The world around them doesn't stop, but they can't see anything. They have their seeing-eye goats, or dogs, and navigate just fine.

Josh was losing his sense of direction. He forgot north and had no idea where he was going. All his faith was in the goat.

The goat, it seemed with Josh's limited goat knowledge, would seek food, other goats and light, right? So he let the goat do his goat-thing.

Minutes or hours later, the goat stopped to eat something. Josh felt around, smelled it … it wasn't spoiled or rotten … then tried some. Vegetables, he thought, probably not trash, but it tasted fine.

Then the goat bounced away, on to another trail.

This went on and on.

Josh tried to think of another plan but what else did he have? This was it.

Another four hundred yards and two thousand steps.

Then Josh tripped.

His mind was off thinking and planning about nothing when something got caught under his feet. He fell chest first and on impact released the grip on his seeing eye goat. The goat bleated or maybe he laughed and ran off, leaving his captor behind.

"Goat!" Josh cried, but he didn't expect the goat to return.

Then a voice spoke to him from the darkness. Josh couldn't understand a word of it, but he was struck by how calmly the man's voice spoke. Comforting? Was he trying to comfort Josh?

"Thank you. I'm alright. My goat got away." Josh realized this was totally idiotic trying to talk to a person from 1400 BC in English but it was dark and the person would probably chalk it up to an illusion or psychoses.

Surprisingly the man kept right on talking, probably to keep his sanity by making a connection in this dark world.

His soothing tone put Josh to sleep. His final thought before dozing off was wishing he wasn't in the middle of the street where he could get run over. But who would be out driving their cart at this time of night?

Then he was out.

? hours – ? minutes – ? seconds
(Darkness)

Hours later? Josh awoke. The darkness made him sleepy setting off the sleep factor inside him. And the man was still talking! Josh listened for a moment then stood, feeling his way around.

"I'm going to go now. I'm not sure where. Take care, okay?"

The voice answered him with more talking. Josh found a wall, and he was gone.

Again, Josh had no idea where he was going but going somewhere just felt good. Better than sitting around and waiting to die. Josh remembered hearing the Jesus freaks talk about these plagues in the Bible and how long they lasted.

A day? 40 days? A year?

Something about three days came to his mind. Seventy-two hours. Josh couldn't tell if they were halfway through that or it had just started. By falling asleep his clock was way off.

You're going to die.

Josh didn't need any more voices talking to him right now. He just needed to find some light.

The drive to move on pushed greater inside Josh. He needed to get out.

This is death.

Moving on past this voice, to somewhere more hopeful.

Death is darkness.

"Stop it! I'm busy here!" Josh yelled out loud.

This is what madness feels like.

Josh's mind was spinning and arguing with itself so much that he forgot about the darkness and taking careful steps.

That's when he fell, headfirst, into a ditch.

Unconscious and out. Again.

? hours – ? minutes – ? seconds
(Darkness)

More time passed.

Josh awoke disoriented, frustrated, lost, confused.

How much longer will this last? Forever?

At this point, Josh felt he had done everything he could to get out of this situation.

You have done everything?.

Had he done everything? He knew what Chen, Maria and her new friend Saleem would say.

Pray.

That won't do any good.

A tug-of-war started in his heart. To pray or not to pray. Josh knew the consequences to himself if he prayed. But who would know? He's just sitting here alone in the darkness.

I would know.

Wait, was this God whispering to him or the other guy? This spiritual life was too confusing and weird. All these voices, how could he tell the difference between God, the devil, and his own voice?

Better to just sit here and wait. It will all be over within a day or two.

But God if you can hear me…

Just then, a hand touched Josh's chest. It frightened Josh, who screamed, but the hand remained, waiting.

"Who are you?" No answer.

"Can you help me?" No answer.

"Can you see in the dark?" No answer.

Panic swept over him. "Bales?" No answer.

Josh had no other options. If it was Bales with his infrared glasses, okay, maybe he'll get to where he needs to be. Sitting here and waiting was accomplishing nothing.

Josh took a risk and grabbed the hand. It lifted Josh to his feet and guided him slowly through the darkness. The hand moved gently a little left then a little right.

The whole process took what felt like an hour.

Josh had no idea where he was going but he just felt a wave of appreciation. "Thank you." His guide still didn't answer.

"Josh!" The voice was very distant but clearly Maria's. The sweetest voice he ever heard.

"Josh!" That was Chen, then Hajj, even Saleem was a welcomed voice.

Up ahead, Josh saw torches bobbing on the horizon in the darkness. His friends had entered the darkness, coming to look for him.

"Over here!" he cried.

Inside, Josh hurried, his mind moving ahead to the reunion and forgetting about the present. He stumbled, falling flat. The hand extended again, helping Josh to his feet.

"Can you see the light?" Maria cried.

"Yes! I'm almost there!" Josh replied. A few more steps and Josh's eyes began to adjust to the light. He could see two torches and made out the faint images of his friends holding those torches.

Josh wanted to push on and run to his friends, but the hand kept a steady pace.

"Don't leave me!"

"We won't!" Chen responded.

Within moments, the hand released him and Josh stumbled forward and fell into his friends' arms. They embraced. Josh never knew a friend's hug could mean so much.

They took a step backwards and passed through a wall of darkness immediately into the light. The light hit Josh so hard, it knocked him off his feet. He writhed on the ground, holding his eyes.

His pain sparked a whimper, then a full-on weeping. Josh cried and cried while his friends held him and comforted him.

Josh cried himself asleep.

72 hours – 16 minutes – 33 seconds (Afternoon)

Josh opened his eyes and could see the Septagon clock. He started to do the math in his groggy head. He had been lost in the darkness and sleeping for well over twenty-four hours. That meant the darkness will still going to continue for another forty-eight hours.

Josh couldn't imagine another forty-eight seconds in that place, let alone forty-eight more hours!

He laid in the tent and heard his friends outside chatting.

A head popped into the tent opening. Saleem. "He's awake!"

Josh positioned himself to receive visitors as they all piled into the tent. The light outside still bothered his eyes but they were slowly adjusting.

Everyone greeted Josh enthusiastically.

"How are you feeling?" Maria asked.

"Good," Josh said, then suddenly felt the need to suppress the emotions flooding the surface. His friends allowed him that moment. "I'm not going to lie … it was scary."

"I can't imagine it," Saleem replied. "Even for the brief moment we peeked into the darkness, it was frightening."

"I know blind people live that way all the time, but to be thrown into it with an entire city and hearing their cries and screams was …"

"Hell." Maria let that sit there.

Josh nodded, totally agreeing. "I've never been in a place where I've felt the darkness."

Then the Lord said to Moses, "Stretch out your hand toward the sky so that darkness spreads over Egypt— darkness that can be felt." So Moses stretched out his hand toward the sky, and total darkness covered all Egypt for three days. No one could see anyone else or move about for three days. Yet all the Israelites had light in the places where they lived.

Exodus 10:21–23

The others gasped, trying to understand the torture he felt.

"Why did you leave us?" Hajj asked.

"I wanted to find Bales. And I saw him."

"What!" they all said together.

"We crossed paths. He talked nonsense trying to be … trying to provoke me. Then he put on these infrared goggles that soldiers use for night vision, just as the lights went out. I tried to grab him, but he got away."

Hajj tapped his forehead with his fist. "We should have thought of that. We should have brought those goggles."

"How did you survive all that time?" Chen inquired.

"I felt around walls and stumbled all over the place. One time I grabbed a goat who had a rope around his neck and used him to guide me. Goats see in the dark, right?"

That broke the mood as his friends imagined that scene in the light. "You had a seeing-eye goat?" Chen chuckled.

Even Josh started laughing. "He was my friend! I want to thank him! Did he come running out before me?"

As the jokes and laughter died down, Josh remembered one other thing. "Someone was in that place with me. He guided me out. Who guided me out of the darkness? Did you see anyone else?"

Everyone stopped, confused by the question.

"Someone guided you out?" Maria asked.

"Yeah, someone took me by the hand and led me to you guys."

Everyone looked at each other, still confused.

Saleem replied. "We stepped three feet into the darkness, which was like a dome over the area, a curtain between light and dark. But we didn't venture very far inside."

"We found torches and used them as lighthouses to guide you home," Chen said. "Nobody walked in and found you."

Josh sat confused. He could have sworn.

"Could it have been the shepherd?" Maria whispered.

Josh believed Maria was right. There really was no other explanation. The thought sparked all his memories. The shepherd who seemed to know him and watched him before and after they traveled to Noah. The shepherd he saw before and after they traveled to Sodom and Gomorrah and who he saw before they left for Moses.

But before this, the shepherd never appeared in the time travel, only on both sides of their time travel—in modern times, in Josh's reality. How could it be him? Did the shepherd have a time travel machine?

Your mind is playing tricks on you. There is no shepherd.

Josh and his friends discussed any updates over the last day. Chen told of talk he had heard amongst the Israelites of God's great power to allow light to happen in one part of town and darkness in another. From what Chen heard, no one had escaped the darkness.

"Have you seen Moses?" Josh asked.

"No," Saleem replied. "This is a big group. But we think we know where he lives. Let's go, we'll show you."

The group crossed through the mass of people. Josh again noticed a stark difference between this town and the town he had just escaped from. Everyone here laughed, sang, and enjoyed the company of one another.

He looked to his left just to witness, again, the strange sight. The entire area looked like a dark curtain stretching for miles, from earth to sky. It's not that a little light bled into the dark area. No light crossed over. Josh kept thinking it looked like the end of a page.

Then his friends stopped. "There," Chen pointed.

Josh saw an ordinary tent. The only thing that stood out was the presence of men around the outside, presumedly guards.

"Doesn't he travel into the city to see Pharaoh?"

"Yes. And we think there is one more time he does. After the darkness, right Hajj?" Chen turned to Hajj who looked unsure, but nodded, approving.

"This next plague is the big one. Very big. And sad," Saleem said mournfully.

"What is it?" Josh really did not know.

Hajj spoke, his voice trembling. "The plague on the firstborn."

There it was again. Josh heard this before, "Firstborn?"

"God will cause death to come to the first born son born in every household."

Hajj's words didn't make sense to Josh when he first heard them. "Wait, the oldest son of every family will die? That's like every house. I'm the firstborn son." Josh was beginning to understand.

"Me too," Chen said.

Hajj raised his hand.

"I have an older brother," Saleem replied. "That's the first time I've been happy about that."

"Why would God kill the firstborn son of every house?"

It was a heavy question. Chen, Hajj, Saleem, and Maria all looked at each other wondering who would tackle that one.

"Well ..." Chen started.

A man walked up to them, holding three loaves of bread. He looked older or maybe just weathered being a human in this day and age. His beard showed some age but his spirits were engaging and kind. He started talking to the group, holding the loaves up. Chen immediately responded graciously and took the bread. Chen then pointed to his friends, saying something that caught the man's attention—something unusual to him.

Chen turned to his friends. "This man just brought us some bread. He's over there in that home and has been watching us. His daughter came by with blankets earlier." Everyone smiled and nodded to the man, who put his hand to his heart and bowed.

"I also told him that you were visitors and you didn't speak the language. He seems interested to know where you came from." Chen waited for an answer.

Nobody had a good answer.

"Tell him Las Vegas," Josh offered. "He hasn't heard of it. It's not a lie, and he has no expectations to who we are."

Chen laughed, then took a breath and responded. Josh could hear the "Las Vegas" worked into the response. The man looked interested. Chen pointed far off into the horizon, like saying, "It's that way."

The man continued talking, pointing toward his home. Chen translated, "He's offering us his home whenever we need assistance." The man bowed then walked away.

"What a nice guy," Maria said.

"Did you get his name?" Saleem asked.

Chen called out a question as the man walked away.

The man responded, "Nahshon."

"We may take him up on that offer, especially if we're still here during the last plague," Chen reminded them. Everyone agreed, except Josh who still wasn't quite sure how the last plague worked. More death he supposed.

72 hours – 16 minutes – 33 seconds
(Night)

The darkness over the Egyptian city continued the rest of the day and into the night.

Josh had wandered outside his tent during the night to see the dark cover over Egypt in the darkness. It was eerily present and real—a big black curtain encircling an entire region. It was something he sure hoped he would never see again in his lifetime.

He returned to his tent, and he was sure he was disturbing the others. His clock was way off being in darkness so long, and he had heard that people in Alaska, where darkness lasted over a month, had trouble sleeping with those long nights.

"Having a hard time sleeping?" Maria whispered.

"Yep. Can you believe we are over halfway through our trip here?" Josh whispered back. Maria was face-to-face next to Josh, but in the tent it was hard to see her. He could smell her she was so close.

"Seems like we should have accomplished more, but it fits the pattern of the other trips. We are waiting for Bales to make the next move."

"He does have one redeeming quality, I must admit. Patience. Right now he's probably hiding in the darkness with his goggles on for three days."

Maria adjusted herself closer to Josh. "Oh, I was thinking that too. Evil is patient, willing to wait to get what it wants. But God plays the long game too."

"Well, these plagues don't show a degree of patience on God's part."

"Oh they do. God has been very patient with this situation. In fact, I love Exodus 34 that says, 'The Lord is compassionate and gracious, slow to anger, abounding in love and faithfulness. He maintains love to thousands, and forgiving wickedness, rebellion and sin. Yet he does not leave the guilty unpunished.' Something like that. God heard the cries of His people, inspired Moses to action, now He's punishing Egypt for their stubborn refusal to let His people go."

"Love and patience to Israel. Punishment and plagues to Egypt," Josh replied. "God sounds a little schizophrenic."

"Well, we don't see everything behind the scenes. We just have to trust that God knows best."

"So what's the reason behind this last plague coming up?" Somebody else stirred in their sleep. Was it just incredible timing or were they listening?

Maria took a deep breath. "It's the most devastating of all the plagues, and it will cause, or force, the Israelites out of Egypt."

"Killing every firstborn son could mean a huge percent of the population?"

"Hard to say. But God gives them a way to protect themselves."

"How's that?"

"They have to slaughter a lamb and put the blood on the doorframes of their houses. Those who believe in God and His message will then be protected. Those who reject Him sadly will not."

Josh processed this unusual request by God. "How does lamb's blood keep the firstborn safe?"

"God will tell Moses that death will pass over each house that sacrifices a lamb and puts the blood on the doorframe. It's why it's called Passover."

"Right, but how …?"

Saleem chimed in. "I don't know if there's a 'how' answer but a 'why' answer."

"Are we keeping you up, Saleem?"

"Sort of, but it's an interesting conversation. The reason the people are safe is because they do what God has told them to do to be safe. The lamb's blood shows obedience and trust."

"It's also symbolic," Chen chimed in.

> "On that same night I will pass through Egypt and strike down every firstborn of both people and animals, and I will bring judgment on all the gods of Egypt. I am the LORD. The blood will be a sign for you on the houses where you are, and when I see the blood, I will pass over you. No destructive plague will touch you when I strike Egypt."
>
> Exodus 12:12–13

"Oh, now everybody's up? Hajj are you with us too?"

"Yes," Hajj replied meekly.

Chen continued. "It's symbolic because in fourteen hundred years from now Jesus will represent that same 'lamb of God' and die for 'the sin of the world.' If you believe in Him, then death will 'pass over' your life."

"Why the firstborn son? What's so special about him?"

"Good question," Saleem said, jumping in. "The firstborn son always represented the next generation of the family. The hope. The firstborn inherited his father's dynasty. Plus, it points to Jesus later on, who will be the firstborn son of Mary and Joseph. He will die as well, but as a sacrifice for our sins."

"But you have to apply Jesus to your life, just as the Israelites will be asked to apply the blood to their doors. It's a voluntary act of the will," Chen added.

"Okay," Josh wanted to stop the conversation that was getting too spiritual for him. "I assume that means we need to find shelter somewhere when Passover happens."

"My calculations put our departure close to that timeframe. As always, God wants to make it all interesting," Chen said.

"Maybe Nahshon will let us stay at his place," Hajj offered.

Everyone thought that was a good idea.

They continued talking into the night and fell asleep sometime before sunup.

The darkness was about to lift but a new darkness would soon replace it.

64 hours – 9 minutes – 8 seconds
(Morning)

Nobody got much sleep that night thanks to Josh's insomnia, so the team napped and dozed then got up late morning. It was clear that the rest of the city was awake and moving about. But there was something buzzing in the tone of the people outside.

Josh joined the others and could see the entire city was outside their homes and looking toward the darkness. Josh remembered the Fourth of Julys back home and everyone outside to see the distant fireworks. It had that kind of community excitement about it.

"They are waiting for the darkness to lift," Chen told them.

"Has it been three days?" Josh asked.

"In Jewish counting, any part of a day is seen as a day. So the darkness happened around the afternoon making it day one, then lasted a full second day, then when it lifts today, at any time, it will be another day, the third day. It could be this morning."

As Chen spoke, Josh was watching Nahshon and his family—what looked like his wife, an oldest daughter and a younger son—off in the distance. Many people came by to greet and talk with Nahshon. He was definitely popular. Once during his interactions with others, Nahshon turned and saw Josh looking at him. He waved. Josh waved back.

The others followed Josh's eyeline and also waved and bowed to Nahshon who graciously returned all their greetings.

Then a wave swept through the town. Josh felt it too. A gut instinct. A pull. A curiosity to turn toward the darkness. Everyone did and at that moment, silently, the darkness faded, dissolving into light. The entire moment took five seconds.

The city gasped collectively then cheered and applauded.

Josh could feel the darkness, or the memory of it, lift from himself too. The view of the darkness from his vantage point acted as a reminder of his time in the darkness. Now that it was gone, he sighed with relief.

While everyone cheered, Josh looked toward Egypt.

He's waiting for you.

Josh instinctively started walking toward the city. His friends grabbed him and held him back.

"Whoa, whoa, whoa, where are you going?" Maria asked.

"He's in there. He was wearing the infrareds to hide. We have to find him."

"Let's wait a moment until things die down. As you can see, not many people feel the need to travel into Egypt. There's no reason to go there. If we do, it will cause suspicion."

Slowly, people returned to their homes and started their day.

Josh looked into the distance and could see somebody, or somebodies, stumbling toward the city. After a few minutes, he could see a family (father, mother and three children) coming toward them. A couple of men and three ladies from the Israelites went out to meet them.

The family collapsed into their arms. Josh and the others walked toward them as the city performed emotional triage on them. Chen listened to them relay their experience to the others. Josh looked into the traumatized eyes of the father—a hollow, scary look that Josh knew. He understood what this man and his family had just gone through.

Chen relayed the information he just heard. "They were Egyptians in the darkness for three days. They just held on to each other. They crawled around and found a little food and water. Once the darkness went away they left Egypt. They don't want to go back. They know God is the one true God."

As Josh watched Israel adopt this new family from their country, another wave of excitement spread through the camp. Everyone in the team could feel it. Josh could only compare it to the sense of a storm coming into the area, the distant sound of rain mixed with wind told you something was coming.

Only this time it wasn't something, but someone.

Moses.

A small entourage of seven men surrounded a central figure on the inside. They moved with authority. The atmosphere changed, feeling heavy and important. People in their path stopped and fell to their knees, crying out. Josh looked around and his friends were already down. Maria's trembling hand pulled Josh down to join them.

Moses carried a thick staff, nearly his height. His long beard and long hair encompassed his tanned face like a lion's mane. It was peppery grey in color, thick, and it flowed in the breeze Moses created as he walked. He moved well for an old guy, Josh thought.

By his side was another guy, equal in age, also carrying a staff, who had an equal air of authority about him. They looked the same but the beards covered a lot of facial uniqueness.

"Who is that?" Josh whispered.

"Moses, who else," Chen said.

"I figured that. The guy next to him."

"Aaron, most likely. His brother."

"Moses had a brother?"

"Yeah, and a sister too. Aaron was the middle child and Miriam the sister was the oldest. Moses was the youngest. They were all Jewish people born in Egypt."

Josh pressed for more information. "Does Aaron play an important part in this story?"

Chen nodded his head, still thinking. "Yeah, when Moses was first called by God to lead the people out of Egypt, he didn't want to do it, so God allowed Aaron to join him as a spokesman."

Saleem jumped into the conversation. "Also, the line of Aaron produced all the priests who worked in the temple."

"Yeah, that's important too," Chen said.

Josh noticed how intently Hajj was listening to all this, yet saying nothing to blow their minds like he usually did. Josh figured this wasn't a good time for a history lesson so he just kept quiet and watched the rest of the events unfold before him.

Moses and his team walked toward the homeless family, who seemed to know instantly who stood before them. Everyone, including the children, fell on their faces, crying. Moses pointed at them, inquiring.

Someone from the Israelite group who had met them seemed to tell their story to Moses who listened intently. The lack of expression on Moses' face could be interpreted as sternness or concern, Josh couldn't tell.

After a minute of explanation, Moses leaned over and took the hand of one of the children, a girl. He helped her to her feet then placed both his hands on her hands. She was sobbing so much it made Josh choke up. Moses then said something, waved his hand over the family and moved on.

People cheered and acknowledged the word of Moses. The people immediately attended to the family, welcoming them into their family. Moses then marched past the group, following the path the Egyptian family had walked to get to Avaris.

Moses was heading to Pharaoh!

Chen stood and brushed himself off. "That was unbelievable. Moses heard their story and gave approval that they could join the Israelites. Everyone was very excited."

"He's everything and more than what I expected. What authority he commands," Saleem said. Tears were running down his face. "Why am I crying?"

"He's a man of God," Maria said, herself tearing up. "You can feel it."

"He's going to Pi-Ramesses. Another showdown with Pharaoh?" Josh asked.

"The last one," Hajj replied.

"We have to follow them. This is Bales' big chance to take out Moses." Josh waited for his friends who shockingly didn't start sprinting. "Why are you hesitating?"

"We don't know Bales' plan," Maria spoke up. "Maybe it's Moses, but it feels like more than that."

"The pattern has been the big heroes of the Bible—Noah, Abraham, so why not Moses?" Chen responded.

"We just have to be careful. Evil has qualities we expect and it behaves within certain patterns, but it's not so easily defined." Maria sighed. She pointed to Moses. "We have over two days left here. Bales' big move probably won't happen until after that. But I say, let's follow them, even for just the sake of curiosity."

The others agreed, thankful for Maria's permission. Everyone immediately started following Moses through the desert.

It became clear that nobody else from the city seemed interested in the encounter that was about to happen. Maybe after nine plagues they were just used to it. Maybe, Josh thought, they just trusted Moses.

Either way, Josh knew Bales was lurking around, most likely in Pi-Ramesses.

58 hours – 28 minutes – 17 seconds
(Afternoon)

As Moses and Aaron entered the city, the guards ran.

In fact, everyone ran when Moses walked down the streets. Men and women audibly screamed when they recognized who was coming.

Chen said the people cried, "Another plague!"

Moses never flinched or checked out the surroundings, looking neither left nor right. He was singularly focused on a crash course with Pharaoh.

Josh and his friends kept silent, watching the heavyweight champion enter the ring—the court of Pharaoh.

Anyone dabbling around Pharaoh's throne ran for their lives. Only a few close to him stayed, and they definitely looked scared.

Pharaoh sat up in his throne, preparing for another round with Moses. He waved Moses past the remaining guards who bravely stayed to protect their king. Once dismissed, they too ran out of the room.

Pharaoh's first words to Moses were not friendly. Moses responded in a tone that wasn't angry but definitely firm. Pharaoh didn't like the response and wrapped his head in his arms.

Chen slid the group to the back of the court so he could translate. "Pharaoh said to Moses to go and worship the Lord, saying everyone could go but to leave their flocks and herds behind."

"That's weird," Josh said. "Why doesn't Moses take the offer?"

"Pharaoh keeps making demands, trying to stay in control. Moses won't stand for it. He wants the animals to go because they will be food for the Israelites and also part of the sacrifices they make to God."

"Moses should just give in," Josh replied.

"No, Pharaoh should just give in. He's not the one calling the shots." Maria's statement resonated with the others.

Pharaoh wrestled emotionally on the throne. The pressure was so much, he stood and paced. His hand gestures and arm movements looked like he was literally, physically wrestling with himself—knocking his head, gritting his teeth, biting his lip, punching his chest.

Then he screamed a response. Everyone jumped in the room … except Moses who seemed to expect the response. Pharaoh added a final statement and waved Moses off. The Egyptians in the room gasped.

Moses stared at Pharaoh, not moving. Josh wondered if he was listening to another voice in his head.

Chen translated the obvious, "Pharaoh said, 'no way' and told Moses to get out of his sight and if he ever came back, he would be killed. Now, I fear, Pharaoh has set in motion the final plague."

Moses took a deep breath, then stroked his beard. Calmly he replied to Pharaoh, turned on his heels and headed for the door.

"Moses just said, 'I'll never see you again,'" Chen whispered.

But Moses stopped before he left. His face was red hot. He screamed something so blood curdling that everyone stopped what they were doing and held their breaths. The impact of his statement sent Egyptians to the ground, wailing, waving off Moses to leave them.

Pharaoh stood on his throne. His body showed defiance but his face lost all color. It was the look of doom.

Josh thought if the expression "dropping the mic" was ever relevant in this day and time, Moses' off-stage departure defined it. He marched off with his crew.

> But the Lord hardened Pharaoh's heart, and he was not willing to let them go. Pharaoh said to Moses, "Get out of my sight! Make sure you do not appear before me again! The day you see my face you will die." "Just as you say," Moses replied. "I will never appear before you again."
>
> Exodus 10:27-29

Moses passed by the team on his way out. For a moment, Moses, normally focused and single-minded, looking only straight ahead, turned and stared straight at Josh.

Josh felt his breath exit his body.

But Moses kept walking, returning to his straightforward path.

"He just looked at you," Saleem whispered.

"What did you do?" Hajj asked.

"Nothing." Josh finally swallowed, which his normal bodily functions forgot to do. Moses seemed to peer into Josh. It was similar to the feeling he got with the shepherd.

"What did Moses say just now," Saleem asked Chen.

Chen waved the team to follow Moses. "Let's keep up with Moses, and I'll tell you along the way. It's not good."

The team followed a safe distance—fifty feet or so—behind Moses' entourage. The Egyptians in the streets continued to run to safety as he passed.

Chen translated Moses' words of doom on the Egyptians. "As you can tell, Moses was red hot. He said at midnight every firstborn son in Egypt will die. Pharaoh had told him to never come back again and

Moses confirmed that he would never see Pharaoh, that this was the last time."

Maria took a deep breath. "It's happening."

"It's amazing," Saleem said, "that with everything that has happened, Pharaoh still held his ground. The man is stubborn."

"Like Bales." Josh was watching the tops of buildings for a glimpse of Bales. If ever there was a good time to take out Moses, it would be right now, in enemy territory.

"Yes," Maria replied. "Evil is stubborn."

Right then, as if on cue, Josh saw him. His head popped up from a second story. Just as Josh felt the words, "It's him" in his throat, a man from the crowd nearby cried out and began running toward Moses and the others with a knife in his hand.

Josh, barely thinking, put out his foot and tripped the man, who fell forward, his legs wrapped up in his cloak, hitting his head on a rock. Blood immediately poured out from the cut.

The disturbance did not catch Moses' attention, who kept moving forward, but a few in the streets saw what happened. Josh looked to the roof again, but Bales was gone.

"Bales was there on the roof!" Josh said, running around the building, looking left and right. He banged on the door of the house and when the people answered, Josh burst in. "Where is he?" The people looked terrified and completely confused by the strange man shouting a strange language at them. Josh found his way to the second floor, but no sign of Bales.

Josh exited, apologizing to the family, who hid under a table, the children crying. Josh felt bad and tried bowing to see if that helped. It didn't.

Back out in the street, the others tended the wounded man on the ground.

"Did you find him?" Maria asked.

"No, he got away." Then Josh saw the bloody man on the ground, who was sitting up and looking pretty good except for the blood all over his face. "How is he?"

"Better now that God used Saleem to heal him," Maria said.

"He confessed that he was trying to assassinate Moses and that a man fitting Bales' description hired him, promising him safety for his family and the city," Chen added.

"I'm sorry he got hurt," Josh sort of apologized.

"No, it's okay," Chen said. "He was grateful you stopped him. We told him the God of Israel healed him. He seems interested in knowing more."

"Well, at least Moses is okay and back on friendly territory," Josh sighed relieved. "Let's get back there."

They left the grateful, healed would-be assassin and followed the path back to the Avaris.

They knew the worst was yet to come.

52 hours – 9 minutes – 42 seconds (Evening)

As the team arrived in the Israelite village, the people were gathering in a centralized location. Word apparently had gotten out about Moses' final encounter with Pharaoh. They wanted news and instructions. Hundreds of thousands of people filled the streets.

Josh and the others were on high alert now, especially after the assassination attempt. They pushed through the crowd, trying to find Moses and Aaron. Judging by the direction people were facing they found him. He stood on a rock that elevated him four feet. His voice boomed as he shouted to the people. Every word he spoke, others turned and spoke to others so the verbal magnification of information spread in all directions.

Josh leaned into Chen who translated.

"He said the negotiations with Pharaoh failed. He will not listen to our request to go and worship the Lord in the wilderness. His heart is hard. The Lord told me that was the last time I will speak to Pharaoh. Now a final plague will release us."

A ripple of cheers spread out. Moses paused to let it be expressed.

"Now he said I will give you more instructions tomorrow but right now, God wants you to go to the Egyptians ..."

Josh could hear the groans. "They won't like that."

Then Chen brightened as Moses continued, "And ask them for their gold and silver. God will impress them to give you all that they have!"

The people went nuts. It was like one million people had just won the lottery.

The mob of a million Israelites walked briskly toward the Egyptian city.

Chen added, "They are very happy."

As they followed, Josh stated, "This looks like an invasion."

"It sort of is, but a God-led one," Maria replied. "The Egyptians will surrender voluntarily."

"After nine plagues of attack and especially the final three days of darkness, the Egyptians will be thrilled to get the Israelites out of their peripheral," Hajj said. Again he answered truthfully but not confidently like he used to. Josh patted him on his back, thanking him for that information.

> The Israelites did as Moses instructed and asked the Egyptians for articles of silver and gold and for clothing.
>
> **Exodus 12:35**

As the sun set over the city, Israelites walked every square block of Pi-Ramesses, knocking on doors. Politely and with smiles on their faces, they addressed their Egyptian neighbors. The Israelites entered their houses then walked out with jewelry, precious items, and coins. It was like a Halloween trick-or-treat with treats of gold!

The Egyptians practically dumped everything they had into baskets and cloaks, giving them to the Jewish people who knocked on their doors. When the Israelites could carry no more, they returned to their homes.

"These people have been slaves for so long," said Saleem. "Now they are getting gold and silver for their hard work probably from the very slave drivers who bossed them around. This must make them very happy."

Josh couldn't wrap his head around the voluntary surrender. The sounds of clinking and clanking filled the streets with laughter and cheers—obviously all from the Israelites.

Josh turned and was startled when an old woman stood in front of him with a gold bracelet. He refused it but she insisted. The others encouraged Josh to take it. So he did, probably thanking her a little too much.

The old woman disappeared in the crowd. Josh thought the bracelet looked expensive and put it in his pocket.

Everyone else in the group was offered something and took what they received.

"Now," Josh wondered, "this jackpot is nice but don't they have to carry it through the desert where it will be useless. There's no premium outlet malls along the way."

"That's true," Saleem replied. "But all this gold will go toward the construction of the tabernacle."

"What's that?"

"The portable temple they will construct in the wilderness. Plus some of that gold will go toward the making of the ark of the covenant."

"And the golden calves," Hajj added.

> "Tell the people that men and women alike are to ask their neighbors for articles of silver and gold." (The LORD made the Egyptians favorably disposed toward the people, and Moses himself was highly regarded in Egypt by Pharaoh's officials and by the people.)
>
> Exodus 11:2-3

Saleem agreed. "Yes, and sadly, the golden calves."

"What golden calves?" Josh still didn't get all this biblical talk.

Saleem continued. "The people will get scared when Moses disappears to the mountain to talk to God for forty days. They will turn from God and build two golden calves as idols and worship them instead."

"Look, I don't get this whole God thing but worshipping two golden calves makes absolutely no sense to me at all," Josh laughed.

"You mean like those?" Maria pointed to a little altar area someone had built. Around a platform were flowers and ashes where something was burnt. On the platform was a small golden image of a cow.

Chen got a closer look. "This is how the Israelites got that idea."

"Well, let's take it." Josh reached over and grabbed the golden cow.

A man's voice cried out to them. The group turned to see three men with spears pointed right at them. The man spoke.

Chen translated. "The man said we can have anything in his house, but don't touch his gods. I think it means a lot to him."

Josh smiled uncomfortably and set the cow down. Everyone backed off.

"Moral of the story ... Don't mess with someone's god," Maria whispered.

"No kidding," Josh agreed as they all slipped into the crowd.

The team followed the Israelites back to Avaris. Everyone was in a festive, happy mood. That night people sang, told stories, and laughed, jingling their rewards, wearing them proudly. Some modeled their new accessories. It was a fun night for all, the kind of laughter Josh and the others hadn't heard since the soccer game in Beth Shemesh.

Nahshon came by with bread, vegetables, and a little meat and everyone partied until late into the night.

"This will be the last night of festivity for these people," Saleem said. "Things get pretty serious after this."

"Tomorrow, Moses will tell them what will happen, and they will prepare for the first Passover," Hajj told them taking a bit of warm soft bread.

As the group went to sleep, Josh kept wondering what Bales' plan in all this was. So many people were around, it was hard to find him—and, with all these people around, it would be hard to take Moses out. One lesson Josh learned from Sodom and Gomorrah was that Bales never did what you expected.

Josh had to be ready for anything.

40 hours – 33 minutes – 51 seconds (Morning)

The team woke up hearing a disturbance outside, an unsettled rustling of spirits. Maybe the people were tired from the all-night partying, but something was happening. Everyone could tell.

Many of the Israelites were outside their tents and slowly shifting east. The migration felt important but not yet urgent. Josh and the others allowed the crowd to determine the pace.

Along the way, they enjoyed the generosity of the community. They received water and bread for breakfast. Some still wore their Egyptian prizes on their bodies. All this bling looked out of place and kind of funny. Like a 14th Century BC rap convention.

Then the group began to congregate in a mass around a tent that sat alone in the center of this community. No other house or construction was near it by a hundred feet or so.

A man stood outside the tent looking straight ahead. Josh thought he recognized the guy. It was Aaron, Moses' brother.

Chen picked up on the buzz. "That's Moses' place. Everyone is getting ready for him to speak."

Josh picked up on the immensity of this entire community. He only saw one portion where he slept but this was massive—like hundreds of thousands of people. They were mostly men who came to hear something then to return to pass along the information to their family.

Josh thought the tent looked like it was … glowing? It wasn't a bright light nor was it like a ray beaming through the clouds. It came from within. If it were night right now, Josh thought, the tent would definitely be lit up.

After an hour of patient waiting, the crowd stood at attention when the tent flap curled back and Moses stepped out. He took his time and straightened his cloak, carrying his staff by his side. For eighty years old, Moses certainly carried himself like he was thirty.

Everyone immediately hushed.

Moses' first line caused a ripple of shocked gasps.

Moses waited until everyone calmed down.

"What did he say?" Saleem asked.

Chen could hardly get the words out. "At midnight, the firstborn son of every Egyptian will die, from Pharaoh to the slave girl."

Moses commanded the stage, speaking loudly and boldly, decisively and purposefully.

The people listened intently as if their lives depended on it—and it did.

As Moses started, Chen turned to the group and said, "This is a lengthy download, most of it I remember from the book of Exodus. Instead of talking all through this, let me summarize it later."

Everyone complied, then Josh had an idea. "What if we use this time to split up and walk through the crowd? Maybe Bales is hiding in here somewhere."

The others agreed, reluctantly. Someone always got in trouble when they split up. Chen stayed put and listened. Maria and Saleem went one way and Hajj and Josh went another. Josh wanted to go with Maria, but realized Hajj would probably feel more comfortable around Josh.

As Josh and Hajj walked through the crowd, they had to pretend like they were listening to Moses but just repositioning themselves. They didn't want to show any disrespect to this man that everyone held is the highest regard.

But also, they wanted to look at the faces of the crowd, not staring awkwardly at them to create any suspicion. Thankfully, very few hid under scarves. Their faces were fully exposed but there were literally hundreds of thousands of them!

The extent of the crowd shocked Josh even more as he moved further and further into it. Hajj looked overwhelmed probably because of his size in this mass of adults.

Josh started thinking about the ancestors that would descend from these people. If just one of them died prematurely, over 3,000 years of ancestry died with them. The calculations of those possibilities began to distract Josh. His mind forgot the mission—to find Bales.

Was that him?

Josh stopped and looked twice at the man who had the facial features of Bales, but when he realized Josh was looking too long at him, he turned to Josh and flashed a friendly smile.

Definitely not him. Maybe an ancestor?

Moses said something that stirred the crowd with murmurs of reverence. Josh and Hajj kept pressing through.

After what seemed like an hour, they returned approximately to where they started. As Josh scanned the crowd, he noticed someone staring at him. It frightened Josh until he realized it was Nahshon, his friend. His eyes and face showed concern, maybe for Josh or maybe for the others.

Josh nodded, not knowing why, and Nahshon nodded back.

Then suddenly right over Nahshon's shoulder, Josh saw Bales.

Bales looked right at Josh. Time stopped for Josh. While Nahshon looked at Josh with concern, Bales looked at Josh with hate.

Now what are you going to do, smart guy?

The voice reminded Josh that he really had no plan. He was on a seek-and-find mission but had no idea what to do once he found.

That's when Bales pulled out a gold dagger, probably Egyptian. Bales looked ready to stab someone but Josh caught him in the act. Instead of hiring someone to do the work for him, Bales was going to do it himself.

Suddenly, Moses shouted something from the stage and the crowd replied with a deafening reply of solidarity. All hands went up and cheers went out as if their team just scored a touchdown. The moment shocked Josh, who jumped to look around and see what happened.

Then, everyone in the crowd fell to their knees, bowing down and calling out. Only Josh and Bales remained standing. Josh wanted to charge Bales but the worship service didn't seem like a good time. Quickly, Josh fell and pretended to worship also.

Moses finished his message, stepped off, and returned to his tent.

Josh jumped to his feet and Bales was gone. The people began to dissipate returning to their homes.

"What is it?" Chen asked, getting up from his worship posture.

Josh pushed through the crowd. His emotions were a little too highly charged for this gathering as people were somberly returning to their homes. Josh pushed one or two innocent bystanders to the side, as he tried to get through the crowd.

Josh felt a hand on his shoulder. He turned thinking it was Bales ready to stab him and saw Nahshon who looked at him with a worried expression. He said something which Josh didn't understand. Josh shook his head, took a breath then, not really knowing what to do, hugged Nahshon with a big bear hug. Nahshon slowly patted Josh on the back. Josh looked Nahshon in the eyes, who seemed confused by the affection. Josh smiled, released him then moved on.

He calmed himself, moved gingerly through the crowd, keeping a watchful eye for Bales. But too many people were moving and scattering in all directions. Josh squeezed through and was pulled by the crowd. After ten minutes or so of getting nowhere, Josh remembered Hajj and he looked back.

Hajj wasn't with him. The poor guy was only three feet tall or so and couldn't see over the crowds and probably got lost. Josh struggled for a second, whether to seek out his enemy or his friend.

Maybe Bales has him!

The thought created urgency in his steps. Josh retraced his movements looking for Hajj, but there was no sign of him. He couldn't shout his name or it would create unwanted attention. Finally, after what seemed like forever, he found Hajj.

Hajj was kneeling in front of Moses' tent.

Josh panicked. Hajj was not in a healthy mental state to be drawing attention to himself, especially to the big guy Moses. Hajj could expose them all as threats. Josh had learned that the Israelites were very particular about outsiders and this could get them kicked out.

Bales had an advantage over them—he was alone. Josh wondered if he himself could do more if he wasn't slowed down by the others. There were only five of them now. How would they operate with SEVEN?

Then again, the translation skills of Chen, the healing power of Saleem, the wisdom of Maria, and the knowledge Hajj brought to the group made them pretty incredible. Right now, one of those team members had completely lost faith in himself. Josh knew exactly how Hajj felt.

Josh walked toward Hajj hoping to escort him back to their home base with the others, but was cut off by the sudden appearance of Aaron, who stepped out of the tent and saw Hajj. Josh stopped, pretending to be distracted by something, keeping an eye on the situation.

Aaron curiously studied the little boy on his knees, his hands extended. From this distance, Josh couldn't tell if Hajj had his eyes shut or he was crying. Aaron was drawn to Hajj's circumstance, walking to him.

For a moment, Josh couldn't tell what Aaron was going to do—have this intruder removed or ignore the kid's moment of repentance. Maybe Aaron didn't know what to do either.

Aaron placed both of his hands on Hajj's head and prayed. Hajj's body jolted as if electrocuted, his hands raised up to the sky. The one-minute prayer ended when Aaron lifted Hajj's chin and looked Hajj in the eyes. Hajj nodded in agreement with whatever Aaron said, then Aaron left him, returning to Moses' tent.

Josh scrambled over to help Hajj who was smiling and crying.

"Aaron just prayed for me."

"Or something like that." Josh helped Hajj up and somehow they found their tent. The friends all welcomed their lost friends, now found.

Josh had waited for this moment to ask Hajj what happened and what Aaron said to him.

"I remembered everything that you guys were saying that I needed to make sure I was close to God before I could be expected to be used by God. That location by Moses' tent felt like a place where God visited, and I wanted to be there. I could feel His presence, so I bowed to my knees to worship God. It was incredible. Then Aaron …" Hajj teared up, his lip quivering. "Then Aaron, I guess, prayed for me. I didn't understand a thing he said but my spirit did. It felt like electricity going through me."

"I saw how you reacted when he touched you," Josh confirmed.

"Yeah, it was amazing. I can't believe that happened." Hajj choked up again, then sobbed. Josh found himself embracing his friend as he cried. People passed by wondering if everything was okay. Josh smiled and nodded at them.

After a moment of taking it all in, Chen began to speak. "Moses gave some pretty sobering instructions at the meeting today."

"It was about Passover, right?" Saleem asked.

"Yes. I know you probably all remember what it was about but hearing it from him, in his voice, was devastating. I could tell it hurt Moses to talk about it."

"I don't know what it's all about. What's Passover? I only see the food in the grocery store designated for Passover. Jewish people celebrate it, right?" Josh wondered.

The rest looked at each other, sensing the foreboding spirit of death they were about to communicate.

Chen took a breath. "Moses told them at midnight, God will strike down every firstborn son living in Egypt. Every one of them will die."

"All of them?" Josh asked. It was still hard to fathom.

"Every one of them. Even the firstborn male of a cow will die."

Josh crinkled his brow. "That seems a little much. What did the cows do?"

"It shows the power of God," Maria countered.

Chen waved his hand. "We're jumping ahead and time is running out. Moses said there will be a loud wailing of crying tonight throughout the land but nothing would happen to Israel if they followed his instructions."

"Tonight?" Maria repeated.

"Yes, tonight. Everyone has to get ready. Moses went over the schedule. Tonight they must take a lamb for their family. The lamb must be a year-old male without defect, and it must be slaughtered when the sun sets. Then they must take some of the blood of the lamb and put it on the sides and tops of the doorframes of the houses where they live and then cook and eat the roasted lamb inside their homes. He told them not only what to eat but also to be ready."

"Ready for what?" Josh asked.

"Ready to leave Egypt. They are getting out of here tonight."

"Tonight?" Josh repeated.

Chen nodded. "It's happening fast. What happens tonight will be what the Israelites celebrate for a few thousand years to come. It's a big deal."

"And Bales will certainly want to ruin it," Josh said.

"Wait," Maria cried. "If the plague happens tonight, we have to be in a house where a lamb was sacrificed. Where is that?"

Nobody had an answer.

"Moses did say a family can share and eat with others in the same house." As Chen said that, they heard a happy humming pass by. It was Nahshon carrying wood. As if right on cue, he stopped, looked at them and said something. Chen replied enthusiastically, smiling and tapping his chest. Nahshon went on his way.

"Guys, Nahshon just invited us to his house for dinner tonight."

Everyone sighed in relief. "Thank you, God," Maria expressed.

"Should we bring an appetizer or something?" Josh asked.

Everyone laughed.

28 hours – 8 minutes – 29 seconds
(Early evening)

Josh checked the time on the Septagon carefully hidden in his bag. The next few hours he felt were going to be chaotic. Outside the sun was setting and, according to Chen, the people needed to start getting into their houses.

Josh joined the others as they watched the events unfold outside around them. One sound began to be heard over everything else.

The protests of the lambs.

People passing either carried a lamb fighting to get free, or walked a lamb casually to their home, or tucked a compliant lamb over their shoulders. Every lamb was going to be dead in an hour and some of them seemed to know it.

Nahshon tied his lamb to the door of his house. The lamb bleated in protest to being tied up, looked around, then accepted its fate, finding scraps and crumbs to nibble on—its last meal.

Nahshon's little son came out and began to pet the lamb. Josh never caught his name but he was a cute kid, like six years old or so, definitely younger than Hajj. While the lamb may not know what was about to happen to him, Nahshon's son did. Josh thought he saw him wipe a little tear away.

Josh found Chen. "Do you know who Nahshon's son is?"

"His name? No. I'll ask." Chen walked over to the little boy, made some comments then asked him a question. The little boy responded. Nahshon's wife stepped out to see who was talking to her son. She smiled at the friendly exchange and Chen returned to Josh. "Salmon."

"Like the fish?"

"No," Chen overemphasized for effect, "SAL-mun. Not SAM-mon."

"It's the same spelling."

"Whatever," Chen said playfully throwing up his hands.

After a few moments, Nahshon came out with a knife and a bowl. Josh called out to the others who joined him.

This was going to be hard to watch.

Nahshon grabbed the lamb who suddenly seemed to understand what was about to happen. As the lamb kicked and screamed, Nahshon quickly laid the lamb's neck over the bowl and, without hesitation, killed the lamb, its blood trickling into the bowl. Josh winced, looking at Maria who also didn't like the scene they had just witnessed. Only Saleem looked unaffected, then he explained.

"I've seen this before. It's hard but necessary."

The lamb kicked and squirmed, but Nahshon held firm, as he looked up to the heavens, most likely praying. The lamb's cries and kicks calmed until it was clear the lamb was dead. The whole process only took thirty seconds.

Nahshon's hand that clutched the lamb was soaked with its blood up to his wrist. Then, satisfied that he had enough blood, Nahshon set the lamb down. Salmon crossed over to look at the dead lamb, patting it gently on its little forehead. Josh couldn't tell if the boy was crying.

Nahshon then took of bunch of dried plants, tied together in a bunch. The ends were bristled, like a big paintbrush. He crossed to the doorframe of his house, voiced a prayer then, using the crude brush, dipped into the bowl, and wiped the blood on the doorframes, left then right, then put some blood on the upper beam. The blood dripped down the sides and from the top to the ground below.

"What is the brush made of?" Josh wondered.

"Hyssop," Chen replied. "Moses said they had to use hyssop."

Nahshon stepped back and looked satisfied at his work. His wife joined him then they took the lamb and began to prepare the meal. A number of pots were boiling water over the fire.

> When the LORD goes through the land to strike down the Egyptians, he will see the blood on the top and sides of the doorframe and will pass over that doorway, and he will not permit the destroyer to enter your houses and strike you down.
>
> Exodus 12:23

Just as Josh and his friends took a breath after witnessing the slaughter, a huge tidal wave of lamb bleats sounded across the city.

Thousands of lambs all met their death simultaneously. It was a chilling sound that lasted only a few minutes but the chill was felt by Josh for nearly an hour. Following that sound came a murmur of voices.

"Chen, what are they saying?"

Chen listened for a moment. "They're praying. I hear them thanking God and thanking the lamb for giving his life for them."

Soon the smell of roasting meat, boiling vegetables, and bread cooking over the fire began to fill the air. Josh felt himself salivating and his stomach grumbled.

Nahshon stepped out of his house and crossed to Chen. They spoke for a moment then Nahshon returned to his house.

"What did he say?" Saleem asked Chen.

"He said dinner will be served in one hour, and he asked that we take down the tent."

"Why?" Josh wondered.

"Because everyone is leaving Egypt tonight, and he will need that tent for where they are going."

25 hours – 44 minutes – 11 seconds
(Evening)

As the sun set and evening began, the noise of preparation and the chatting of plans slowly died down, replaced by a reverential silence. The smells of roasting lamb still hung in the air, and Maria guessed that nearly 100,000 lambs probably died that afternoon.

Josh believed he heard the cry of each one of them as it was being prepared for this moment.

This trip to the time of Moses contained some of the most horrifying moments Josh would ever remember. While millions died during Noah's ark and around one hundred thousand at Sodom and Gomorrah, their deaths were quick, either by drowning, which Josh barely heard, or fiery impact, which Josh didn't hear at all since he had been running for his life.

These sounds were cried by thousands of lambs (or people). However, the sounds he had heard during the time in the darkness were the worst and would haunt him, Josh felt, his whole life.

"We have until midnight," Chen told them as they folded the tent. "That's about four or five hours from now. Nahshon said to come over soon to eat before sundown."

"So, I've been thinking," Hajj said. Josh was glad to hear Hajj was thinking. "If everyone has to be in a house, covered by lamb's blood, at midnight, doesn't Bales have to be too?"

"Good point," Maria replied. "He's probably making friends—most likely through bribery—and hiding out in their place too."

"Maybe he's not the firstborn male of his family," Saleem said.

"Bales has an older brother? That's scary," Chen replied.

"The Septagon says twenty-five hours," Josh said as he hitched the bag containing their time travel device over his shoulder. "So what will we be here to witness?"

"The final plague, the Passover," Chen thought. "Then the exodus happens right away, so we should be traveling across Egypt. Somewhere along the way our time runs out."

"That's incredible. In like 24 hours, one day, all these people will be free from Egypt and Pharaoh," Maria wrapped the final ropes around the animal hide tent. "God is amazing."

Everyone paused a moment to agree. Josh found God rather like a bully but he kept his opinions to himself right now.

"So we just go into Nahshon's house, hang out and expect Bales to attack sometime during the trip?" Saleem asked.

"I think so," Chen replied.

Josh felt funny going to someone's house without cleaning up, taking a shower, and putting some product in his hair. Nobody seemed to mind that he stunk, but he couldn't imagine he was fun to be around right now. But then again, everyone else was in the same situation.

As they walked up to Nahshon's house, Josh noticed that the blood had dried pretty thoroughly on the door. He then thought about this whole house and how it would just be abandoned as they would never return.

"Do we knock?" Chen asked the others.

Nobody really noticed how it worked around here. Thankfully Salmon opened the door with a big goofy smile. Nahshon and his wife joined them at the door, waving them in.

Josh smiled and bowed his head, which seemed like the way people greeted each other around here. Chen did all the talking, and he made the family laugh. In total, Josh counted five others here—Nahshon, his wife, a teenaged daughter, an older man and Salmon.

Chen spoke to the family, then referenced the other members of his group. He pointed to each one and said something, which the family greeted with surprise and interest.

During all that, Josh looked around at their home and noticed things were packed up on the floor, wrapped in blankets. It appeared they were taking about half the stuff in the house and leaving the other half behind. They were ready to go.

As the family turned to the meal prep, Chen told them what he had said. "I introduced each one of you and said we were all from a land west of here."

"Except me. I'm east of here," Saleem emphasized.

"They don't know that. I said we heard of their great God and wanted to experience Him so we came here."

Maria leaned in, "Who are they?"

Chen pointed to each one. "That's Nahshon, his wife, whose name I didn't get, that's her father whose name begins with a Z, their daughter, who was only introduced by 'my daughter,' and of course Salmon."

"Is Salmon a firstborn if he has an older sister?" Josh wondered.

Chen looked a little stumped. He glanced at Hajj who didn't flinch. "Firstborn son seems to mean either the firstborn of the family or the first-born male of the family."

"So which of all of these are the firstborn sons?" Josh asked.

"Good question." Chen asked them. Salmon raised his hand and so did Nahshon.

Josh shuddered wondering if the blood on the door would really keep them safe. Then again the others seemed to feel safe and knew the story from the Bible much better than he did. Still he was doubtful.

That was his job … to doubt.

The dinner table was a rug on the ground, like an indoor picnic. The food appeared in pots. They sat with a plate in front of them, but no silverware. Three oil lamps lit the room but still things were difficult to see.

Nahshon then directed everyone to sit. Once everyone found their place, Nahshon talked to the group, then raised his hands to the sky, looking straight up to the ceiling. Josh looked at Nahshon's face and his sincere desperation. He looked and spoke as if God was in the rafters looking down.

Josh realized this was a prayer and looked at his friends to see what to do. They seemed confused also as to whether to close their eyes or look up. Salmon followed his father precisely looking skyward with that same love in his eyes. Chen and Saleem also prayed up. Hajj was crying. Maria followed the lead of the women who had their eyes closed. Josh stayed neutral.

Nahshon finished and the food began to be passed. Nahshon talked the whole time.

"He's telling us the significance of the food. The bread was baked without yeast because they are all positive God will free them from Egypt tonight. There's no time to wait for the bread to rise."

The bread was passed and everyone took a bite. There was a purity and wholeness to all the foods they ate here. While it was more like a cracker or pita bread, it was the tastiest Josh had ever had.

Next, the women passed around a bowl with greens inside, like a watery salad. Josh wasn't a big fan of veggies in his world, but here, with so few options, Josh began to like them. He dished out a little on his plate and took a bite.

Yuck. Josh winced as did his friends. Even Nahshon's daughter made a face.

Chen laughed as Nahshon spoke. "Those are bitter herbs. They are to remind the Israelites of their bitter life in Egypt and how God rescued them."

"Couldn't we just talk about it instead of tasting it?" Josh said.

"Makes it more real," Saleem replied.

The course thankfully went quickly followed by the main course, the lamb, roasted well done on the fire. To Josh it looked tasty until he remembered who it was. Images of the playful little lamb tied up in front of the house went through his mind. He fought to keep images out.

Maria smiled at Josh, sensing the same thing. They made sad faces to each other.

Nahshon talked before they ate.

"He's thanking God for the lamb," Chen said, "who gave his life so they could be spared from death."

Nahshon talked a little while. Josh wondered how close they were to midnight, so he opened the bag on his lap to see the time on the Septagon.

22 hours – 38 minutes – 4 seconds
(Evening)

The light shined from his bag and Josh quickly shut it. Hajj looked at him as if saying—*What are you doing*? Josh then noticed that Salmon saw it and was in awe by the mysterious secret. Everyone else in the room looked to the sky and didn't see him.

Nahshon finished his speech then pulled off a piece of lamb and passed the plate. Everybody took a portion and ate it. The taste made Josh forget that dinner had been running around freely earlier today. The plate kept getting passed until all of the lamb was gone. Nahshon ceremoniously took the last bite.

With the meal now finished, everyone pushed their plates to the center of the table and Nahshon began to sing. He had an okay voice, deep and heartfelt. Others joined in when they knew the words.

"Songs of praise," Chen said.

"Yeah, I got that," Josh replied.

The singing went on for longer than Josh expected. Then Nahshon stopped, probably tired from the concert. Everyone sat peacefully and waited in silence. Off in the distance, they could hear other families singing.

In the quiet, those songs sounded like lullabies. Josh noticed Nahshon and others, Hajj and Saleem, started to fall asleep especially in such a dark room. Josh felt like it was Thanksgiving and wondered if the lamb had those chemicals in them like turkey that caused sleepiness.

Josh looked again at Septagon, first making sure Salmon was distracted and didn't see him.

23 hours – 21 minutes – 58 seconds
(Evening)

Just under 40 minutes until midnight.

As the songs circled in the night, Josh heard all kinds of sounds outside—wind, restless animals, creaks in the roof.

A strange sound caught Josh's attention by the door. He looked more closely and saw something seep under the door frame. The light was so dim, it was hard to make out. Josh wanted to ignore it, but something told him to pay attention.

Then it hit him.

Maria screamed in the haze. Now Josh was in this room as a bystander watching Nahshon's wife weep while cradling Salmon who had died in one arm, Nahshon in the other. Maria held Hajj while Chen laid dead next to them. Josh turned and saw his own body, lifeless on the ground.

Then it was over. Josh realized in his vision that he just saw death enter the room. But why didn't it pass over?

Maria was looking intently at Josh. "What happened? Josh? What did you see?"

"Death didn't pass over." Josh looked at the door again. He grabbed a lamp and moved over to the bottom of the door. Definitely a liquid had come through the door. Was it blood?

Josh touched it and looked at his finger. It wasn't red. But clear. Water.

Josh opened the door. Inside everyone sucked air in terror wondering why he would do such a thing.

He held the lamp up to the doorframe.

The blood had been washed off. Josh turned to the streets and caught a quick glimpse of Bales disappearing into the darkness.

"Bales washed the blood off!" His friends knew exactly what he said, but their Israelite hosts did not. Chen told them. Nahshon leapt to his feet in horror and said something.

"He doesn't have any more lambs!"

Josh ran out the door in pursuit of Bales. The streets were empty but it was dark and Josh lost sight of his enemy. In contrast to his predicament, songs of praise filled the air. But right now, Josh had nothing to sing about.

As he turned around, Josh realized he was lost. He took four or five right and left turns and could not accurately repeat them.

"Maria!" Josh yelled.

Voices in the homes responded to the call. A few peeked out their doors wondering who was making so much commotion in this solemn moment.

"Over here!" Maria cried out.

Josh followed the voice.

"Josh!" Maria cried again. "We don't have another lamb!"

Now Josh understood their predicament. He looked around in the darkness, listening for a lamb's bleating. He decided to knock on a nearby door.

The people cracked opened the door. "A lamb," Josh said. "Do you have a lamb?" Josh tried to play a desperate game of charades to describe a lamb but no one understood. The people panicked and waved him away.

Two more doors and Josh realized that was hopeless.

No lamb meant death for five of them.

"Josh!" Maria tried again. She seemed closer.

"I can't find one!"

"The Septagon says there's seven minutes until midnight," she said.

Josh looked everywhere he could but there was no lamb to be found.

"Just come to the house and let's be here together!" Maria's voice seemed hopeless and surrendered to their fate.

Josh realized that may be best. Better to die with others than alone.

As Josh turned a corner, he saw a shepherd. The shepherd. The shepherd he had seen every time he needed comfort.

By his feet stood a lamb. The shepherd smiled and motioned to the lamb to move forward. The lamb walked up to Josh, like a puppy, and laid down at Josh's feet. Josh looked up and the shepherd was gone. Josh wanted to follow him and figure this mystery out, but right now he had to save his friends ... and himself.

Josh grabbed the lamb and turned the corner, finding himself right at Nahshon's house. Maria saw the lamb in his arms and went inside. She returned with a knife.

In the distance, Josh could hear a howling, a cry, not from animals, but people waking up in Egypt to a horrible reality. Death was closing in.

Josh took the knife. The timing made him realize he would have to do it.

Josh laid the lamb down as he remembered Nahshon doing, but the lamb did not fight him. It was compliant ... willing. This made it even harder for Josh to kill him.

"Josh, hurry," Maria cried.

Josh did what was needed.

The lamb did not cry out.

It was so quiet, Josh looked down to make sure he hit the mark. He had. Blood dripped into the bowl. Josh looked around and found the old hyssop brush Nahshon had used earlier.

In the distance, a mile away it seemed, Josh could hear the screams, then more screams—deep, prolonged wails of grief coming from the Egyptian city. Josh stopped because the sound haunted him.

"It's coming toward us," Maria said.

Josh felt the pressure suddenly. His hands shaking. He dropped the hyssop branch. It was dark and hard to find.

You're not going to make it.

He hated that voice.

You deserve to die.

Shut up!

Josh found the hyssop, dipped it in the lamb's blood and began to paint the door frame, left, right, top.

You don't have enough blood on it for your sins.

Josh wondered if that was true and began applying as much as he could. The bowl seemed to have more than enough blood and Josh threw as much on the door frame as he could.

Something like a low-pressure system began to press toward him. He could feel the air shift. Josh looked outside in the darkness.

He could barely make out what looked like a soft curtain brushing across the town, like the darkness, only colder. The sight of it awed him, and he forgot where he was.

Suddenly a pair of manly hands pulled him in and slammed the door shut.

> At midnight the Lord struck down all the firstborn in Egypt, from the firstborn of Pharaoh, who sat on the throne, to the firstborn of the prisoner, who was in the dungeon, and the firstborn of all the livestock as well. Pharaoh and all his officials and all the Egyptians got up during the night, and there was loud wailing in Egypt, for there was not a house without someone dead.
>
> **Exodus 12:29–30**

Josh fell into the room and crashed into the dinner plates. Everyone held their breath as the curtain of death passed over them.

Josh felt it pass through him but not harm him. Like a chill. Like a warning.

Once it safely passed, everyone exhaled. Nahshon, Salmon, and the others patted Josh's back. Maria hugged him. Saleem laid on the ground praying. Hajj joined the group hug.

"What happened," Chen asked.

"I saw a dampness grow under the door and realized it was water. When I opened the door, I saw Bales running away and knew that he had washed the blood off the door."

"You chased him?" Hajj asked.

"Yeah, it's always my first instinct, isn't it, but I lost him in the darkness."

Saleem got up from his prayers. "How did you find the lamb?"

Josh took a moment, wondering if he should tell them. They already thought he was crazy with all these visions. Now this.

"I turned a corner and there was this lamb right where I stood. It was good luck."

Never mention "luck" to a Christian crowd. They all looked at each other with that knowing look.

"It wasn't luck, Josh," Maria pointed out the obvious.

Chen translated the information to Nahshon and his family who looked deeply confused and appreciative.

Then Josh wondered, "Why wasn't Bales wiping the blood off Moses' door? Doesn't he want him dead?"

"Moses isn't the firstborn male. Aaron is his older brother," Saleem said. "Obviously, Aaron isn't significant in Bales' plan. Maybe he was trying to get us off his trail."

Josh noticed Hajj thinking and processing everything. He got very quiet.

Everyone joined in silence but outside there was no silence. The wailing echoed from Egypt. Josh remembered the sound of wolves howling and how it triggered other wolves. The sound always sent shivers through his body.

This sound was worse, because Josh knew those crying were mourning a death in their homes.

A faint rattling sound of metal accompanied by horse hooves was heard in the distance.

"What is that?" Josh asked.

"I bet Pharaoh is summoning Moses," Chen said.

"Maybe this is when Bales will strike. We have to follow them." Josh jumped out the door again. Chen, Saleem, Hajj, and Maria followed him, leaving Nahshon's family behind.

22 hours – 2 minutes – 37 seconds
(Evening)

Josh and the others arrived at Moses' tent, then saw his entourage in the distance walking toward Egypt. They quickly caught up to them, but, as usual, kept their distance, about ten yards behind.

The march into Egyptian territory was not pleasant, even in the night which covered much of the horror around them. However, the darkness could not hide the smell and the sounds of death.

Along the way, they walked by dead cattle. Other cattle stood around their dead family members sniffing their corpses.

Chen explained. "Remember, Moses said even the firstborn of the cattle will die."

It was a disturbing sight especially mixed in with the horrific moan coming from the city. The cries of mourning were sometimes screams of realization and sometimes long wails of heartache. The crying ranged from sniffles to the inability to catch one's breath.

Chen shook his head. "It's heartbreaking."

As Moses walked through the streets, those Egyptians who were outside ran for their lives. Others fell down on their faces sobbing. Moses, Aaron, and a few others kept their focus on their destination.

A few dead bodies lay in the streets, attended to by family members.

They entered Pharaoh's court. One guard laid dead at the entrance while the other was gone, presumedly home mourning his own loss. A few other dead bodies were scattered about the courtyard. Josh had to step over one.

Pharaoh sat on his throne with his dead son in his arms. Standing before Moses, Pharaoh tried to look proud and in control, but his tear-soaked eyes and quivering lip showed otherwise. A woman, most likely his wife, writhed on the ground while her attendants tried to calm her.

Moses and his crew marched in. Chen translated for his friends.

"See what you have done," Pharaoh said.

"I warned you," Moses responded. "Your hard-heartedness brought this about."

Pharaoh did not deny that, then said, "I have decided to let you go. All of you. Get out of my country. Get out of my presence. JUST GET OUT!" Pharaoh lost control then stopped to get himself under control. He continued. "Get up and leave my people. Go, worship the Lord as you requested. Take everything. Your flocks, animals, everything you wanted. Just go!"

Pharaoh collapsed sobbing. Moses said nothing and turned to walk out.

Pharaoh's wife realized who was in the room and screamed, running toward Moses. If not for her attendants, who knows what she would have done. As her people wrestled her to the ground, Moses looked at her with sadness.

Then Pharaoh perked up and called out something. When Chen told them what it was, Josh couldn't believe it.

"Bless me before you go!"

Even Moses couldn't believe it. He shook his head, then turned, and walked out.

Pharaoh took that affirmation positively like everything was going to be okay now.

"So arrogant," Maria said. "Always trying to find an advantage for himself. After all he did, Pharaoh wants to be blessed."

"In a day or so, he'll send chariots after the Israelites so he's not completely sincere," Hajj reminded them.

The group made their way out of the palace, which felt more like a mortuary, and caught up with Moses. The Egyptians in the streets began to make their way outside as word of Moses' arrival spread. They were shouting, not angrily, but passionately.

Chen relayed their cries. "They are telling Moses and the Israelites to go. Get out. To leave. They have definitely had enough of all this."

As they passed one family, Josh's heart broke. A boy held his father, dead in his arms. He cried and looked to them for help. Josh had to look away and move on, but after a few steps heard Maria shout. "Saleem! No!"

Saleem stared down at the boy, sharing in his sorrow.

Maria reiterated. "Saleem!"

"I can help," Saleem cried.

Now all the friends had returned to Saleem.

"There will be grave consequences if you do," Chen said. "That man was supposed to die in this plague. If he lives, you have no idea what his descendants will do."

"You don't decide who lives or dies. God does." Maria said this then glanced at Josh knowing exactly what just went through his mind. She was right. Josh thought about his mom.

"But God gave me this gift to heal. Maybe it was for this moment."

"We are here to stop Bales from changing the course of history," Hajj said. "You're doing the same thing."

Saleem didn't seem to be listening as his hand stretched out toward the dead man. Maria looked at Josh wondering what they should do. Josh thought he needed to physically restrain Saleem from helping someone, which seemed like an odd reason.

Saleem's hand touched the man.

"Saleem!" Chen cried.

The man ... did nothing. Saleem looked surprised. He tried again. The man remained dead. The boy looked at Saleem wondering why he was touching his father. He pushed Saleem's hand away.

"It didn't work," Saleem whispered.

"You don't decide how to use your gift," Maria said. "God does."

Everybody felt a presence was in the circle. They all looked up.

It was Moses, curious over what was going on. Saleem quickly pulled his hand back. Moses nodded then said something to the man next to him. The man waved them all on and the entourage moved on.

Maria pulled Saleem away, putting her arm around him as he cried. "I just wanted to help him." Maria consoled him as they left the city.

Josh noticed Chen was a little disturbed by something while they walked and went back to talk to him.

"You okay?"

Chen looked in awe or confused. "You remember that man Moses just talked to?"

"Yeah, the one who led them out of the city? Yeah, what about him?"

"That was Joshua."

"Nice name. So? Who's Joshua?"

Chen looked at Josh, almost offended he didn't know, then seemed to remember.

"That's right. I forgot that you don't know. Well, he's just another great man from biblical history. I'll tell you about him later."

Once out of the Egyptian city and into the Jewish sector, Moses, Aaron, and Joshua cried out to the people, who then cried out to other people, who in turn cried out to others.

Chen let his friends know what was being said. "Let's go! Pack up! It's time! Grab your things! We're out of here!"

Everyone scrambled, grabbing what they could, while cheering their fate. Families poured out into the streets with their kids, belongings, and animals. They took only the bare necessities and everyone needed to carry something, from the oldest to the very youngest. Mothers swaddled their babies in blankets tied around their chest, while carrying their kitchen on their backs. Fathers guided the animals with their staffs while carrying tools and bedding. Donkeys were so loaded with stuff it looked like they would tip over. Even the smallest children carried something attached to their little bodies.

"This chaos is the perfect time for Bales to strike. Everyone is very distracted." The group agreed with Josh as they were all swept up in the mass exodus to leave Egypt. "Let's make our way to Moses. He's probably toward the front of all this."

As they walked east, the sun began to rise.

15 hours – 47 minutes – 32 seconds
(Morning)

The friends skipped, slipped, and pushed their way toward the front of the mass and found Moses leading the way. By his side were Aaron and his family, a woman Hajj said was Moses' sister Miriam and her family, and Joshua who they saw earlier.

It was unclear the destination but they just moved toward the fresh morning horizon. Josh tried his best to get a perspective on the crowd.

When he looked back or climbed a rock, he saw nothing but people covering the landscape.

No wonder, Josh thought, Pharaoh was so upset over this slave force leaving his country. Now the Egyptians would have to do all the hard work themselves!

How is Moses going to feed all these people? Where are they going to get new clothes? What kind of shelter will protect them?

The questions started piling up in Josh's mind. Better to leave them alone. He was sure his friends had an answer from the Bible.

The masses talked amongst themselves. Some sang songs. Animals bleated and mooed. Josh saw lots of sheep, but very few lambs. He knew why.

Children playfully laughed and chased each other. Josh remembered the excitement of going on a trip with his family. Those first few hours filled with anticipation were replaced by the grind of a sixteen-hour drive ahead of them. Josh believed the reality of this trip would soon set in and not everyone would be in such a great mood.

Josh listened carefully and believed he could hear the ground thumping as the million plus people caused a moving earthquake with every step. This had to register on a Richter scale if one had been invented.

Josh suddenly found himself standing knee deep in a red river. It was silent. All Josh could hear was the trickling of water.

Coming toward him was a woven basket floating on the water. Slowly it made its way toward Josh.

The basket revealed a baby inside. So cute and angelic, no crying it made.

Josh couldn't help but smiling. By instinct he reached out to tickle the little one for a smile.

But as he did, a giant claw reached out of the blood-red river and pulled the baby underwater.

Josh stumbled and fell to the ground. The others grabbed him and picked him up.

Maria knew. "What's up? What did you see?"

Josh slowly pieced it together. "It was like my first Noah vision. This time it was a baby. On a bloody river. A claw pulled it under."

"Moses? But his whole incident with the basket on the Nile happened eighty years ago," Chen said. "Why would you have a vision that looked back on that?"

"Maybe it's a premonition that Moses will die?" Saleem asked. "But we all know he dies in forty years."

Maria's mind was racing. "Josh's vision looks to the future or something happening right now."

"A drowning?" Chen thought. "We are heading to the Red Sea eventually. I think it's like three to five days away."

"Yeah, maybe Moses will drown in the Red Sea," Josh concluded. "That makes sense."

Everyone seemed to be on board with that idea.

Except Hajj who stared off into the distance. "Where's Nahshon?"

"Nahshon," Josh replied. "What does he have to do with anything?"

"We have to go find him." Hajj began to walk against the crowd, back toward Egypt.

"Hajj! What about Moses?" Saleem cried out.

"It's too early to say but I don't think Bales is after Moses."

Hajj sprinted off against the flow of traffic. "If we find Nahshon it will confirm what I think is happening." The others exchanged looks to each other, then ran after him.

"Do we follow him?" Josh asked.

"He hasn't been well," Saleem added.

"Yeah, but God's been repairing Hajj and putting him back together. Maybe for this moment," Maria said. "Let's follow him."

It was strange moving against the massive crowd. Many looked at them in shock.

Hajj hadn't been thinking clearly and Josh wondered if they could trust him. But Hajj seemed convinced about something … more confident than ever.

12 hours – 2 minutes – 58 seconds (Morning)

The team arrived back at the Jewish city of Avaris. The city was eerily quiet. Dropped items littered the streets. A forgotten goat wandered around, happily enjoying his freedom.

They entered Nahshon's house. Nobody was there.

"Hajj are you sure?" Chen asked. "Everybody's exiting the country quickly and we're all alone here."

Hajj ignored the question, then stopped to think. Confidently he asked, "Josh, tell us your vision again."

Josh recounted his vision about the river, baby in a basket, and the giant claw.

> Now the length of time the Israelite people lived in Egypt was 430 years. At the end of the 430 years, to the very day, all the LORD's divisions left Egypt. Because the LORD kept vigil that night to bring them out of Egypt, on this night all the Israelites are to keep vigil to honor the LORD for the generations to come.
>
> **Exodus 12:40–42**

"That's Moses. Moses was in the basket," Saleem repeated.

Hajj didn't seemed convinced of that. "Have any of you seen the Nile while here?" Hajj asked. Nobody had. "The place where Moses was dropped in the water had to be nearby and the river then flowed down to the Egyptian city we were just in. Let's keep moving west."

"But … ?" Maria asked but she was too late. Hajj ran to the door. As he opened it, Nahshon's wife stood there crying. Maria grabbed her as she fell into the room, her words mixed with wailing.

Chen interpreted. "Her firstborn son is missing, Salmon. A man took him. Her husband went looking for him and told her to stay in the house."

"Tell her to stay," Hajj replied. "We know where they are." As Chen talked to the woman, she looked hopeful for a moment. "Ask her which way is the Nile?"

As Chen did, she looked confused over such a strange request. She pointed west.

Hajj ran out the door. Chen said something to Nahshon's wife. "I told her to stay, and we will be back with her husband and son."

She cried with joy as they ran out the door.

Hajj was right. Something was up with Nahshon.

10 hours – 33 minutes – 29 seconds (Afternoon)

The Nile was closer to the city than they thought.

And longer and wider too.

The group scanned the river. Reeds covered the banks of the Nile making it easy for someone to hide.

"Look at this!" Saleem announced. Everyone ran to him. Saleem pointed to the red stain along a patch of reeds and water.

"Red when God turned it to blood. But it's almost washed away now," Hajj said. "This way." Hajj ran south, downstream.

As they walked along the banks, pushing through the high grass, Josh asked, "Is there any wildlife around here we should know about?"

"Just alligators. The Nile gator is the most famous," Hajj replied. Everyone stopped on cue and looked around.

Chen, at the front of the line, hesitated. "They probably aren't friendly like on the ark."

A muffled cry was heard. Was it a bird or maybe a frog? Everyone stopped to listen. They heard it again. Definitely human, coming twenty yards ahead.

This time they ran and sloshed ahead, pushing through the grass.

There was Bales, wearing his backpack and fighting Salmon in his arms. The little kid put up quite a fight even with a knife against his throat. Bales saw the others and stopped. He looked annoyed at their constant interruption, then smiled that haunting grin.

Josh spoke first. "Put him down, Bales. You don't want to hurt a child."

"Oh, but I do. The firstborn is the key to everything, haven't you understood that?"

Josh hadn't but he didn't want Bales to know that.

Bales looked deeper into Josh's eyes. "Oh, but you don't understand because you don't believe in God."

"And you do?"

"Oh there's a God. Look around you. Look where we are. How can you not believe? I believe but I just do not bow."

Somehow Bales was making sense to Josh.

"This little boy will make sure I never have to."

Josh could tell that Bales' momentum shifted to action. His arm raised up to bring the knife across the boy's throat.

Suddenly Bales was hit from behind. Nahshon had crept up through the water and attacked the man who was trying to kill his son. Both of them splashed into the water, wrestled and tussled. Nahshon had the advantage since Bales carried a heavy thirty-pound pack on his back.

Bales dropped Salmon who splashed into the water then quickly ran away into Maria's comforting arms.

Bales pointed the knife at Nahshon, ready to stab him. Saleem, Chen, Hajj, and Josh moved toward Bales who quickly realized he was outnumbered. Bales slowly backed away from Nahshon. "Killing you will do no good. I need the boy."

"It's over Bales. You can't have him," Josh said stepping in front of Salmon.

Bales had a second thought. He grabbed Nahshon in a head lock. "Maybe I will kill his father then just so our visit here wasn't a waste of time. Or you can give me the boy and we call it even!" Bales looked serious.

"We'll keep the boy," Josh replied, joining Chen, Hajj, and Saleem to make a wall in front of Salmon, protecting him but also shielding him from what may happen next.

"I wanted God to kill him with those stupid bloody door regulations, but you ruined that plan. What joy that would have brought to see death spread over their house just because they didn't paint a little blood on the frame. Now, I'll have to do what I wanted God to do."

"No!" Josh shouted. Bales looked like he was ready.

But as he lifted the knife higher, something splashed out of the water behind him, grabbing his backpack, pulling him backwards.

An alligator. A Nile one, and he was big.

Nahshon, now released from Bales, ran away toward the others, embracing his son.

Bales stubbornly tried to get his footing, but the gator kept pulling.

"I wonder who sent that gator, mister!" Saleem yelled.

In frustration, Bales looked at Josh. He knew this part of the journey was over.

He reached toward the pack and pushed the button, firing up the time machine on his back. As it roared and whirred, the gator stopped, confused and distracted by what was happening. The Nile gator released his mysterious prey.

"Back up!" Hajj yelled as everyone quickly turned to run to the shore.

Josh could feel the heat rising behind him. "Go! Go! Go!" He pulled Nahshon with him as Nahshon carried Salmon to safety.

Then came the sonic blast and pulsating heat wave. The explosion was mixed with water, like someone just performed a hot cannonball dive. Josh looked back and a mushroom cloud of water rose at the spot. The gator did not do so well. He was cooked, boiled, and fried well done in the process and thrown twenty feet behind them.

Bales was gone. Again.

Everyone stood on the shore, catching their breath. Josh wondered what Nahshon and Salmon thought. "What are you going to tell them, Chen?"

Chen thought for a second then proceeded to explain something to Nahshon and Salmon. Their mouths hung open in disbelief but they appeared to buy the explanation.

"What did you say?" Josh asked.

"I told them that Bales was an evil Egyptian and God took him out in a fiery blast. After all the plagues they've seen, that didn't seem too farfetched."

"We need to get them back to their family," Maria said, putting her arm around Salmon.

"I have a question I want to ask Nahshon," Hajj said. Hajj then walked up to Chen and whispered in his ear.

Chen asked Nahshon the question. Nahshon replied.

As they proceeded east, Josh asked, "What question did you ask, Hajj?"

"I asked him what tribe he was from."

"And he said?"

"That he was the leader of the tribe of Judah." Hajj moved on without any explanation but Josh didn't think he would understand anyway.

Everyone walked back into Avaris and met Nahshon's wife who wept and embraced her little family. Salmon cried too and even tough ol' Nahshon got a little misty.

They walked for a few hours and caught up with the Israelites moving west. Nahshon's family was very appreciative, kissing everyone. The family tried to give them trinkets but everyone refused.

Josh and his friends watched as Nahshon caught up with others and were warmly received. "I can only imagine the story they are telling."

"Well, with everything they've seen recently, nothing should surprise them," Maria responded. "God has been doing amazing things."

The team agreed they should separate themselves from the Israelites since they would need to disappear soon and with all these people around it would be hard to explain. They watched as the Israelites walked off. Josh had never seen so many people moving in unison with each other. He was sorry to see them go. It was like saying goodbye to family.

2 hours – 20 minutes – 6 seconds
(Early evening)

Josh looked at the Septagon. "We have a couple of hours, what should we do?"

"Yeah, this is unusual," Chen thought. "We normally don't have any extra time to just hang out. I wonder what God is up to?"

Chen got his answer. A man called out to them. Everyone turned to see an Egyptian soldier holding a spear coming toward them. Behind him, a few yards back, two chariots pulled up.

"Time to go," Josh yelled as he struggled to pull the Septagon from the bag. Everyone quickly reached to grab the Septagon and make a dramatic exit from the scene.

But the soldier knocked it from Josh's hand and drove the blunt end of his spear into Josh's gut. Josh felt all the wind escape him. The others ran to his aid. The soldier picked up the Septagon and looked it over.

"Hey, be careful with that!" Josh cried. The soldiers looked offended by his tone though they had no idea what he was saying. The one looked like he would hit Josh again, but Josh backed off.

Chen took the softer approach and engaged them in a conversation as five soldiers converged and bargained, looking at the strange device.

Chen shared everything the soldiers said. "They are saying they are spies keeping their eye on the Israelites. They want to know more and think we have that information."

Saleem laughed. "We actually do have that information. We know the whole Bible story."

"They don't need to know that," Chen said as he continued talking to the soldiers. "Uh-oh, they're saying they want to show the Septagon to Pharaoh since they've never seen anything like it before. We have to go with them."

"How much time is left on it?" Maria asked.

Josh tried to see as the guard waved it around.

2 hours – 01 minute – 41 seconds
(Early evening)

"An hour and a half. It's getting dark."

"Let's hurry," Chen said then addressed the soldiers. They escorted them east, thankfully on the chariots which Josh, still recovering from the blow to his stomach, thought was actually kind of fun, but it ate up a lot of time. Josh couldn't see the Septagon but it felt like an hour had passed.

The fun horsey ride ended when they pulled up into Pharaoh's courtyard.

Everything looked depressed and everyone miserable around the ruins of a once beautiful city. The chariots pulled right up the steps, and the soldiers encouraged the team with their spears' sharp tips to move up the steps.

They entered the throne room to see Pharaoh slouched in his throne, depressed and near tears. Josh saw a broken and tormented man before him. It was sort of sad but Josh felt he put it on himself.

The guards told their story to Pharaoh who seemed to perk up. He looked them over and seemed to recognize them. Chen confirmed. "He remembers us and wondered if we were up to something."

"He seems happy now that he has prisoners," Josh quipped. The soldier shoved Josh forward to his knees then pushed a spear into Josh's side. Suddenly this got serious. The one guard handed Pharaoh the Septagon who looked it over with great curiosity. A few shaggy magicians walked up and examined it over his shoulder, trading ideas and possibilities.

Pharaoh spoke to Josh who did not have a clue what he said.

Chen translated: "He says he saw us walking here earlier and believes we are spies working for Moses. The punishment for spies is death."

Pharaoh leaned back in his throne.

"Do we get a trial or maybe hire a lawyer?" Saleem asked.

"Not around here," Hajj replied. "Pharaoh is the judge, jury, and, oh yeah, he thinks he is God."

Pharaoh thought long enough then yelled something to the guards.

Chen screamed, "Look out!"

Everyone was pushed to the ground and spears put to their necks.

"I guess that means no appeal?" Saleem said.

"Nope," Hajj said. "And whatever we do, we can't hurt Pharaoh or keep him from pursuing the Israelites. The Red Sea miracle is one of the greatest in the Bible."

"Maybe killing us is the inspiration he needs to follow them?" Saleem wondered.

"I don't like your ideas, Saleem," Hajj said, nervously choking on his words.

Josh had an idea. "Chen!"

"Yeah?"

"Translate for me."

"Be careful."

Chen translated as Josh spoke. "O great and mighty Pharaoh, king of Egypt and the world, we humbly beseech you to listen to us ..."

Maria chimed in, "That should work. He loves praise."

Josh continued. "We heard of you in our faraway land and traveled a long distance to witness your greatness. This power you faced was mighty and caused much devastation but you are not to be stopped. You must fight, Pharaoh!"

"Oh, I see what you're doing," Hajj commented.

"You must show these Israelites that you are the king of Egypt! Who does Moses think he is? A shepherd coming in and telling a god what to do! This is your time to rise up! Show the world who you are!"

Pharaoh considered everything Josh said and Chen translated.

"I think it's working," Chen said.

"Stand up," Josh told the group.

"You think that's a good idea?" Maria asked.

"We're about to find out." Josh slowly rose to his feet. The guards allowed him to. The others followed. "We have come from the god Ra to encourage you to fight."

"Wait, what are you saying?" Maria wondered.

"We have come," Josh continued, reaching into his bag, "to show you a sign."

"We can do signs?" Saleem wondered.

"Well, you can more than of any of us," Chen replied.

Josh approached Pharaoh and held out his hand, asking for the Septagon. Pharaoh didn't look willing to surrender it, but most likely his curiosity pushed him to give it to Josh.

Josh held up the Septagon with a dramatic pose. The guards stepped back and gasped. Pharaoh gazed with wonder at it. "We will now return to Ra and tell of your greatness. We will tell him that you did not stop fighting the Israelites. We bid you farewell!"

0 hours – 1 minute – 12 seconds
(Evening)

Josh was surprised how little time was left on the Septagon. He turned to his friends. "Grab it now."

Everyone reached out and put a hand on the Septagon. It began to heat up.

"One other thing before we go in case something goes wrong," Hajj said, "I know what Bales is after."

Everyone glanced at each other. This was a heck of a time for a revelation.

"He's trying to destroy the birth line of Christ."

And they were gone.

15

For Josh, everything went dark … again.

He found himself inside a metal coffin, standing upright. Why wasn't he in Avaris, standing in the ruins where he departed—just like he had zipped into time in one spot then arrived back at the same spot again?

Something was definitely up with this Septagon.

Then the dehydration set in. His body physically ached. He wanted water. Needed it. Fast.

Saleem, Josh thought, *forgive me for everything bad I thought about you. You are the most important member of the team!*

Josh didn't know what to do in a coffin, so he screamed.

"Help! Somebody get me out! Help! Where am I?"

Josh could move his feet so he kicked the metal coffin. The noise it made sounded familiar. He had heard it before, but everything was going dark in his mind.

Show no pity: life for life, eye for eye, tooth for tooth, hand for hand, foot for foot.

The voice in his head was getting annoying.

Then Josh thought he heard real voices approaching as he continued kicking, but the kicking was wearing down as his body was giving out. His voice only scratched and moaned.

He was dying.

"I think it's this one!" Josh heard a voice that sounded familiar but it didn't really matter right now. He was dead.

The door opened up and Josh fell into her arms.

As everything started to go black, Josh looked back at his coffin. It was a metal locker.

The floor he laid on looked very familiar.

The sign on the wall announced the coming prom.

He was back at his high school in Tennessee.

And he felt terrible. Where was Saleem when he really needed him?

THE END

THE SEVEN: COLLAPSE

Book 4

CHAPTER 1 PREVIEW

Josh woke up and looked at the posters on the wall talking about hormones, puberty, hygiene, germs, and fungus.

It was the office of the school nurse.

Mrs. Hanson, a kind soul who failed to read some of the nutrition posters on her own wall, waddled in wearing her white scrubs like she was going to do surgery on Josh. She read over a chart in her hand wearing those prescription half glasses attached around her neck with an ornate necklace.

"Josh, why were you found inside a locker this morning? Are there bullies at this campus invading your safe space?"

If she only knew.

"No."

"You were very dehydrated. How long were you in the locker?"

"I'm not sure."

"Did you know these people who put you in the locker?"

"No. Nobody put me in the locker."

Mrs. Hanson looked up over her spectacles. "No one. You put yourself in there? Was it some kind of dare?"

"No, I leaned in to get my lunch and fell in. The door shut behind me. It was a terrible accident." Josh wondered if that was considered a lie. Would the truth be the right thing? Could this lady handle the truth?

"Lunch isn't until an hour from now. You must have been pretty hungry."

Josh was, actually. "Starving. I haven't eaten for thousands of years." It took him a moment to realize what he had just said. Mrs. Hanson's look told him that he had said something wrong. "Thousands of seconds, I mean. Did you know one hour equals three thousand six hundred seconds?"

"Very intuitive, Josh. You must excel in math."

"He's very smart and getting A's in every class," Maria said as she stormed into the room and started to pack up Josh's things. "Josh needs to get to that class right now. The teacher is asking for him."

Josh knew that was her voice he had heard earlier while buried in his metal locker-coffin. Seeing her was such a relief.

"We appreciate you finding Josh and bringing him to us, Maria, but I really should do a couple more tests on him to make sure ..."

"We have a test. A big test! He needs to take it now. I've got orders," Maria said, starting to help Josh to his feet. Josh wobbled still unsure about his footing.

"Okay," Mrs. Hanson said, unconvinced. "Did you bring a note?"

Maria got Josh out into the hallway just far enough away from responding to Mrs. Hanson's request. Josh had to lean on Maria to keep steady.

"What happened?" Josh couldn't wait to exit. "What are we doing back here?"

"Let's get outside, and I'll tell you what I know," Maria said. Suddenly she pushed Josh into a janitorial closet that was left open. She quickly shut the door. Once again, Josh found himself in a tight, confined space. At least, this time, he was with her.

"What are you ..." Josh said as Maria silenced him. Then Josh heard what got Maria's attention. The sound of two men in heeled shoes marched down the hallway. Once the sound passed, he asked, "Are they after us?"

Maria poked her head out the door. "Who knows? I don't know." She motioned him forward. They slipped out of the school right as the alarm sounded indicating the end of another period. Once again, they were leaving school behind.

"How long have you be here in whatever time period we are in?" Josh asked as they began the familiar walk home.

"I'm not sure. I arrived in Big Mike's office and drank a gallon of Gatorade I found in his office. I was walking out and heard you calling from inside the locker and helped you out. As the nurse looked you over, I went searching for the others. I can't find them."

"Big Mike?"

"No sign of him. When I asked, people said he was on leave. They said he was part of the Army Reserves and called into active duty."

"Well, that's true." Josh now understood Big Mike's cover. "But what about our families?"

"Yes, I want to head to my house and yours right now. Maybe we can get some answers there."

"I don't know what's up with that Septagon. We normally get dropped off in time right where we left. Something's falling apart. I don't like it."

Maria agreed. "Yeah, I agree. It's not happening like it has the last three times we traveled through time, but God has a purpose for everything. I have to believe He's behind all this and we are here for a reason."

"I don't know. Something feels funny … off. I don't like it."

Maria stopped walking and looked Josh right in his eyes. "I know it's scary. I'm scared too. But you have to trust in the Lord with all your heart and lean not on your own understanding. In all your ways acknowledge him, and he will make your paths straight."

She's crazy.

Josh had trust issues especially with this God Maria kept pushing on him. So far, he hadn't been very trustworthy with a dead mom and a missing dad all because of a crazed doctor who kept slipping in and out of time, and out of their reach, using Josh's dad's own time machine. Trust was a problem.

Maria had a backpack she had "borrowed" and filled it with drinks, which she shared with Josh as they walked for over an hour. Josh started to feel better with electrolytes and blood circulating in his body. He really wanted to take a four-hour nap.

They arrived on Josh's and Maria's street. Josh's home was closest so Josh stopped in there first. Maria couldn't wait to get her house so she went ahead.

The front door to Josh's house was unlocked and Josh entered. "Hello?" It felt good to be home, a place Josh started to accept as his home even though he had nothing but bad memories here. No one answered. The house was empty. He looked in the fridge. The food was the same as he remembered it when he left, but Josh could tell some time had passed. From the best of his observation, seeing the presence of cobwebs in the house and the expiration dates on the food, six months or so had passed.

Josh examined the whole upstairs, especially his dad's room, hoping there would be some sign of him. Nothing. He had not been here.

There was only one other place to look, a place Josh didn't want to go, the basement—his dad's laboratory.

Josh found a broom and wielded the handle like a light saber, remembering the two bullies Bales sent to rough them up, looking for the battery that made the time travel machine go. He was ready for anything right now.

"Hello?" Josh warned anyone downstairs before they got "broomed" to the head. No answer. So he turned the lights on and crept down the stairs slowly.

The basement was just as he had left it. Even the police tape was still there from the crime scene. The place brought back all the feelings of that day—realizing his father was missing, the stolen inventions, and the thought that Josh was now all alone.

Josh felt his house had turned up nothing of significance, so he left, shutting the door the best he could with a broken latch. He wasn't worried about anything getting stolen. Nothing in that house really mattered anymore except a few trinkets. Bales had everything he needed so why worry.

The yard looked good, acceptable. Thankfully they were entering the cold months so the grass didn't grow much and he believed Maria's family took it upon themselves to keep the outside looking presentable.

Josh crossed the street to Maria's house. He opened the door and found Maria kneeling on the floor, crying. She looked up at Josh and said, "They're gone."

THE SEPTAGON CODE

Can you find the Bible verses hidden in these chapters? They all point to one book in the Bible.

Chapter 1 – _____

Chapter 2 – _____

Chapter 3 – _____

Chapter 4 – _____

Chapter 5 – _____

Chapter 6 – _____

Chapter 7 – _____

Chapter 8 – _____

Chapter 9 – _____

Chapter 10 – _____

Chapter 11 – _____

Chapter 12 – _____

Chapter 13 – _____

Chapter 14 – _____

Chapter 15 – _____

EXPLORE MORE ABOUT MOSES AND PHARAOH

Bible: Exodus 1–13

Who was Moses?

https://www.gotquestions.org/did-Moses-exist.html

https://armstronginstitute.org/692-youve-heard-israels-version-of-the-exodus-have-you-heard-egypts

Who was Pharaoh?

https://www.gotquestions.org/Pharaoh-of-the-Exodus.html

https://www.osirisnet.net/tombes/artisans/neferhotep6/e_neferhotep6_01.htm

Archaeological evidence

https://biblearchaeology.org/research/chronological-categories/exodus-era/4919-top-ten-discoveries-related-to-moses-and-the-exod

https://answersingenesis.org/bible-characters/moses/searching-for-moses/

https://www.smithsonianmag.com/smart-news/first-foreign-takeover-ancient-egypt-was-uprising-not-invasion-180975354/

https://www.biblicalarchaeology.org/daily/biblical-topics/exodus/exodus-fact-or-fiction/

https://www.patternsofevidence.com/2017/12/01/
severed-hands-uncovered-at-avaris/

Check out the films in the Patterns of Evidence series including "Exodus" by Timothy Mahoney

Videos about Mount Sinai

https://www.youtube.com/watch?v=QGttUn5Oe5w

https://www.youtube.com/watch?v=RLVG4itue7E

https://www.youtube.com/watch?v=YkGWuCzZ28I

https://www.youtube.com/watch?v=kaZZP4XjqDo

Facts about Nahshon:

He was from the line of Judah:

from Judah, Nahshon son of Amminadab; Numbers 1:7

He was a leader:

On the east, toward the sunrise, the divisions of the camp of Judah are to encamp under their standard. The leader of the people of Judah is Nahshon son of Amminadab. Numbers 2:3

The one who brought his offering on the first day was Nahshon son of Amminadab of the tribe of Judah. Numbers 7:12

... and two oxen, five rams, five male goats and five male lambs a year old to be sacrificed as a fellowship offering. This was the offering of Nahshon son of Amminadab. Numbers 7:17

The divisions of the camp of Judah went first, under their standard. Nahshon son of Amminadab was in command. Numbers 10:14

He (and Salmon) was in the line of David:

Amminadab the father of Nahshon,

Nahshon the father of Salmon,

Salmon the father of Boaz,

Boaz the father of Obed,

Obed the father of Jesse,

and Jesse the father of David. Ruth 4:20–22

He was in the line of Jesus:

Ram the father of Amminadab,

Amminadab the father of Nahshon,

Nahshon the father of Salmon,

Salmon the father of Boaz, whose mother was Rahab,

Boaz the father of Obed, whose mother was Ruth,

Obed the father of Jesse,

and Jesse the father of King David. Matthew 1:4–6